A Year
Without
Rain

A Year Without Rain

D. Anne Love

Holiday House • *New York*

Library of Congress Cataloging-in-Publication Data
Love, D. Anne.
A year without rain / D. Anne Love. — 1st ed.
p.   cm.
Summary: Her mother's death and a year-long drought have made life
difficult for twelve-year-old Rachel and her family on their farm in
the Dakotas, but when she learns that her father plans to get
married again, it is almost more than Rachel can bear.
ISBN 0-8234-1488-4
[1. Family life—South Dakota Fiction. 2. Frontier and
pioneer life—South Dakota Fiction. 3. Remarriage Fiction.
4. South Dakota Fiction.] I. Title.
PZ7.L9549Ye   2000
[Fic]—dc 21   99-35825
CIP

For Graham
and Caroline

Contents

A Year
Without
Rain

1

A Matter of Time

All summer long we watched and waited and wished for rain. Every morning, Pa and John Wesley and I searched for clouds in the washed-out sky, but each day dawned like the one before, brassy and hot. Our fields dried up and blew away. The green river turned to a brown trickle. No birds sang.

In the evenings, after I had tidied the kitchen and put away our dishes, we sat with the doors open to the heat-thickened prairie twilight, and Pa read aloud from the newspapers that came by train from the East.

"The '96 elections aren't far off," he said one night, turning up the wick in the lamp. "It says here the Populists are campaigning for drought relief. It says they just might win."

"Can they make it rain?" John Wesley asked me, raking his sleeve across his damp forehead.

"Of course not, you little goose. Nobody can make it rain."

Pa's paper rustled as he set it aside. "The folks in Washington are talking about payments, son. Cash money for the crops we're losing. I've never been one to rely on handouts, but if this drought goes on much longer, we won't have a choice."

About a week later, on a breathless July morning, a fire started in the meadow. Through the window, I saw thick gray smoke curling up, and orange flames licking at the brown stubble.

"Pa! Rachel! Come quick!"

Arms and legs churning like a windmill, John Wesley charged up the dirt road with Jake, our old retriever.

I dropped my sewing basket and grabbed the empty feed sacks we kept in a pile on the porch. Pa left the sheep pens and met us at the creek that wound through the cottonwoods behind our house.

We dipped the sacks in the creek and ran into the field, beating back the flames. Back and forth, from the creek to the field we ran, until our legs felt wobbly as a newborn lamb's, and our smoke-blackened hands were blistered and sore.

At last, the fire went out and we stood there on the parched grass, too tired and too discouraged to speak. Even John Wesley, who usually had plenty to say, was quiet.

"That was close," Pa said finally. "We're lucky we didn't lose the house."

"When will this drought end, Pa?" John Wesley asked. "Is it *ever* going to rain again?"

Pa ran his hand over his sooty face. "That's a good question, son. But I reckon the Lord Himself is the only one who knows the answer."

It was a pure wonder Pa had any religion left after everything that had happened to us on the Dakota prairie. The spring I was eight, my mother died, and we buried her beneath a grove of poplar trees on a rise down the road. That summer, a tornado blew the roof off our house and we had to sleep in the barn till Pa fixed it. When I was ten, a blizzard swept in and froze our cattle to death. Then, last April, Pa took sick with a fever that raged for nearly a month, and the neighbors had to help with the spring planting. Now summer had come, bringing an endless drought that sucked out our breath, and our hopes along with it.

John Wesley bent down to scratch Jake's ears. Our old dog stood quietly, panting in the heat. We started up the path toward the house carrying our wet feed sacks.

"Look!" John Wesley said. "A wagon! Coming this way."

We stood in the road while the wagon, brimming with pots and pans and rakes and tables, creaked toward us.

"It's the Walkers," Pa said.

"Looks like they're going on a trip," John Wesley said.

"Whoa!" Mr. Walker stopped the mules in the road and pushed his hat to the back of his head, eyeing the damp feed sacks in our hands. "You been fighting fires, too?"

Pa nodded. "I can't ever remember a time when we've gone a year without rain. It's so dry a person can might-near start a blaze just by looking at the ground."

"That's a fact," Mr. Walker said. "Polly here was doing the washing this morning. One little spark flew up, and the next thing we knew the whole house was afire."

Mrs. Walker blinked her watery, red-rimmed eyes and twisted her hands in her lap. Annie, their little girl, burst into tears. "Our house burned up. And all my toys, too."

"We lost everything, except what you see on this wagon," Mr. Walker said. "Everything we worked for all these years, up in smoke."

Pa shook his head. "I'm sorry to hear that, George. What are you going to do?"

"We're leaving for good," Mr. Walker said. "I can't ask Polly to take any more of this."

"But what about your land?"

Mr. Walker snorted. "A few more days of this heat and wind, and there won't be enough dirt left to plant a potato. It's blowing away faster than I can water it down. The well's dry anyway. We knew we'd lose the house sooner or later. It was just a matter of time."

"Where will you go?" Pa asked.

"Minnesota. Polly's got kin there. Maybe we'll raise dairy cattle. Or I'll find work in a store."

"You'll never be happy working for somebody else," Pa said, squinting up at him.

Mr. Walker shrugged. "Anything's better than this."

Pa looked out at our dried-up fields, the sheep standing listlessly in the sun, the heat waves shimmering on the horizon. "I know it looks bad now, but this drought can't last forever. The papers say there's help on the way, if we can hang on till election day."

Then he said to Mrs. Walker, "It'll be a bit crowded, Polly, but you're welcome to stay here for as long as it takes to build your house again."

"That's neighborly of you," Mr. Walker answered, "but our minds are made up. We're going to Minnesota."

Pa nodded. "Well, good luck to you, then."

Mr. Walker picked up the reins and the harness jangled. The mules stamped their feet, and the dust swirled into my eyes.

"Wait!" John Wesley yelled.

None of us had seen him leave, but now he came running out of our house, and handed Annie a fuzzy blue bundle.

"It's my old bunny," he told her. "His name's Baxter. You can keep him. Since your toys got all burned up."

I stared at him. Our mother had sewed that rabbit for him when he was just a baby. He'd slept with it every night of his life.

"Are you sure, John Wesley?" I whispered. "The Walkers are going clear to Minnesota. You'll never see Baxter again."

"I know it. But I'm all grown up now. Annie's still little. Besides, I have other toys."

"That's mighty kind of you, John Wesley," Mrs. Walker said. "I'll see that Annie takes good care of him."

Annie had already made friends with Baxter. She rocked him and hummed a little tune under her breath.

"Well, we'll be off then," Mr. Walker said to Pa. "Take care, William. Good-bye, Rachel. For your sakes, I hope this blasted drought ends soon."

"Me, too." Pa slapped the mules' rumps and we watched till their wagon was just a dark speck on the horizon.

"Well, that's that," John Wesley said. "Pa, what did Mr. Walker mean, a matter of time?"

Behind his spectacles, Pa's eyes were serious. "It means if we don't get some rain soon, we'll all lose our farms. The way folks are moving out, this part of Dakota will soon be deserted."

"Will we have to move to Minnesota, too?" John Wesley wiped his face on his shirt sleeve.

"I hope not, son," Pa said. "We'll just have to wait and see." He smiled down at us. "Come on now. Let's see if there's any water left in the well. I could do with something to drink."

We turned back toward the house just as a black buggy came trundling up the road.

"What now?" Pa said. "I sure hope it's not somebody else leaving us behind."

"It's Miss Burke!" John Wesley said. "I wonder why she's coming clear out here. Do you reckon the schoolhouse burned down?"

Pa chuckled. "Don't sound so hopeful! I doubt your teacher would come all the way out here just to give you the news in person."

The buggy rolled into the yard and Miss Burke got out, smiling despite the dust and the cruel heat. "Mr. Blackmon! I'm so glad I've found you at home."

Pa wiped the grime off his face and raked his fingers through his hair. He smiled at her, and just like that, all his worry lines were erased, like a cipher from a slate. "Good morning. What brings you out this way?"

"I wanted to speak with you about the school vote next week."

"Let's go up to the house and get out of this heat." Pa handed John Wesley his sacks, and we walked back up the road to the house. Jake lay down in his favorite spot under the porch. Pa and Miss Burke sat in the parlor, and I poured water for everyone.

"Thank you, Rachel." Miss Burke took a long swallow and set her glass on Mama's white china tray.

To Pa she said, "I'm worried. I thought I'd convinced enough people to vote for extending the school term, but in the last week, three more families have moved away. And now, the Walkers! I met them on the road just now, headed for Minnesota."

"They lost their house this morning," Pa said.

"We nearly lost ours, too," John Wesley said. "It was scary."

"What am I going to do?" Miss Burke said to Pa. "With so many families moving away, there won't be enough money coming in to keep the school open for four months next term, let alone five."

Pa rubbed his chin the way he always did when he was thinking. "You could offer advanced classes and charge extra for them. French lessons, maybe. Or Latin. Anybody planning to be a doctor needs Latin."

"Unfortunately, there aren't too many budding doctors in these parts," Miss Burke said. "Most people want their children to know reading and writing, and maybe a bit of arithmetic. I'm afraid they aren't too interested in having them learn more than that. Why, just last week Mr. Norton told me he won't be sending his boys back next term. He said too much learning makes young men restless."

"I suppose," Pa said.

One at a time, Miss Burke smoothed the pleats in her skirt, till they lay just so. "Frankly, I can't see the point of taking a vote next week."

"Nor can I," Pa said. "I'm sure the board would just as soon wait till this drought ends and folks are back farming the land again. I'll speak to them tomorrow."

"Thank you," Miss Burke said, her gray eyes shining. "I knew I could depend on you." She stood up. "I should be going."

We followed her out to her buggy. Reaching inside, she handed me a stack of books. "Since the future of our school seems so uncertain, I decided to bring you these, so you won't fall behind."

"That was kind of you," Pa said. "I'll see that she reads them. And John Wesley, too."

"Me? Why should I have to study when school is out?" John Wesley asked. "I thought this was vacation."

The sound of Miss Burke's laugh was like a sleigh bell on a cold winter night. Clear and pure. Pa smiled as I sifted through my books.

There were two books by Mark Twain, and a book called *Uncle Remus, His Songs and His Sayings* by Mr. Joel Chandler Harris. There were six copies of *St. Nicholas* magazine, my very favorite. They smelled of ink and chalk dust, and the wood smoke from the pot-bellied stove that kept our schoolroom warm in winter.

Miss Burke climbed into the buggy and tucked in her skirts. "The next time I'm out this way, perhaps we can talk about what you've read, Rachel. It pains me to think your education might suffer on account of this awful drought."

Pa put his hand on my shoulder. "I won't let her fall behind. You can depend on me."

"Yes." Miss Burke looked thoughtful. "It's the one thing that comforts me out here. I'm grateful to you."

"Don't think anything of it," Pa said. "I know things look bad now, but I have a lot of faith in the future. Once we get the telephone, and Mr. Edison's electrified lamps out here, the sky's the limit."

Miss Burke smiled. "Your enthusiasm is contagious, Mr. Blackmon. I certainly hope it's justified." She picked up the reins and clicked her tongue to the horse. "Good-bye, everyone."

"I'll stop by after I've spoken to the school board," Pa told her as the buggy began to move. "Try not to worry."

We followed Pa back to the house. John Wesley slipped his hot little hand into mine. "What will happen if it doesn't rain, Rachel?"

"You heard Pa. We might have to move away. But I don't want to."

"Me neither." He blinked against the glaring sun. "What do you reckon it's like in Minnesota?"

"I have no idea. Don't even think about it."

But he did. We all did. If rain didn't come soon, we'd lose our farm. It was only a matter of time.

2

A Long
Journey

The days of summer passed, each one hotter and drier than the one before. The sheep stood panting in the parched grass, too weary to move. In the withered fields the cornstalks rattled like bones, and the wind swirled the dust into a brown fog that seeped in through the cracks in our house. After a while, even the insects stopped their singing, the fireflies stopped their glittering, until it seemed the whole prairie had stopped breathing, waiting for rain.

One night Pa sat us down at the table, and I knew what was coming, even before he told us.

"I've written to your Aunt Agatha down in Savannah," he said. "She's agreed to have you visit for a while."

"For how long, Pa?" John Wesley looked worried. There was a picture of Aunt Agatha in our mother's album, but we had never met her.

"Not for long," Pa promised. "Just till this weather breaks."

"Will you come, too?"

Pa shook his head. "Somebody's got to stay here and watch out for the animals and the farm."

"Won't you be awful lonesome without us?" my brother asked.

"You bet your buttons I will," Pa said. "But I'll have Jake for company, and you'll write to me every week, won't you, son?"

John Wesley nodded glumly. "Jake will miss me, too."

"No doubt. But we'll let him sleep with one of your socks. That'll keep him happy till you're home again." Pa said to me, "I've bought tickets for the train leaving Thursday. I'll expect you to watch out for John Wesley on the trip."

"I can watch out for myself," John Wesley declared. "I'm almost ten."

Pa grinned. "All the same, I expect you to mind your sister."

"All right." John Wesley turned to me. "As long as you don't get too bossy."

Pa shifted in his chair. "I wish we could stay together, but in another few days the river will be bone dry, and I must look for water to keep the animals alive. I might be gone a long time."

"We don't mind," John Wesley said urgently. "Me and Rachel can stay here and take care of things till you come back."

"I'm afraid that's much too big a job for the two of you, especially now that most of our neighbors have left."

His voice trailed away and a worried frown creased his brow. "You must be careful about strangers on the train, Rachel," he said. "You and John Wesley stick together. Keep your money in a safe place, and find the conductor at once if trouble comes."

"I'll be careful, Pa."

Pushing back his chair, he stood up. "Come along, now. I'll help you pack."

We each took a trunk. John Wesley packed his marble collection and the lucky stone he found in the river, and his coin bank with the clown painted on the side, even though it was empty. I packed the books Miss Burke had brought, except for the one about Uncle Remus, which I kept out to help pass the time on our long journey. I took the picture of Aunt Agatha from Mama's album, in case I needed some help in finding her once we got to Savannah. Last of all, I packed a small canvas and my paints, my wrinkled tubes of red and blue and green and white.

"I was hoping you'd take those along," Pa said, handing me the black-handled brushes he'd given me for my twelfth birthday in April. "You'll find plenty of pretty scenes to paint in Savannah. I saw a lot of wondrous places when I was in the Army, but Savannah was the most beautiful." He smiled a remembering kind of smile. "But then, that may have been because your mother was there."

He folded my blue shawl and laid it in the trunk. "I miss her still."

"Me, too, Pa."

"I imagine you do. I know it's hard, growing up without a mother for guidance." Behind his spectacles, his eyes went dark with tears, and he made a funny noise deep in his throat. "Is that everything?"

"Hey, Pa!" John Wesley called down from the loft. "Can I take your pistol, in case we run into Indians on the way?"

"Certainly not!"

"But what if they attack the train?" John Wesley clambered down the ladder and looked up at Pa, his expression serious.

"There hasn't been any Indian trouble around here since statehood," Pa said. "You'll be all right."

"But what if they *do* show up?" John Wesley persisted. "What if they shoot us with arrows and rob us? What if they scalp us?"

"You've been reading too many Wild West stories," Pa said. He smiled down at John Wesley. "Did you pack your socks?"

"Yep. Three pairs."

"Only three?"

"Well, I figure we won't be gone more than three months."

Pa rolled his eyes. "Lord save poor Agatha. She has no idea what's about to hit her."

"What's she like, Pa?" John Wesley asked.

"I haven't seen her in many years," Pa said. "But when I was courting your mother, your aunt Aggie was full of mischief. She liked to play jokes on us."

"What did she do?"

"Well, one time, she hid your mother's shoes just when we were about to go dancing. And one time, she made a cake out of pasteboard and covered it with real chocolate icing. Then she waited for me to taste it. She thought the entire prank was quite amusing."

"Mama would never do things like that," I said. "Mama was serious."

"Yes. She was the quiet, artistic one," Pa said.

"Everybody said so. You got your talent for painting pictures from her. It's a gift."

"Did I get a gift from Mama, too?" John Wesley asked.

"You sure did. Your mother was curious as a cat. Interested in everything, and afraid of nothing. Just like you."

John Wesley nodded solemnly. "I'm pretty brave, all right."

Pa chuckled. "And modest, too. Go finish your packing. It's nearly time for bed."

When Thursday came, we got to the train station an hour early. Pa tied our team of Morgans to the hitching rail and carried our trunks inside. The agent checked our tickets and handed them back to me. "Keep these handy, young lady. The stationmaster will need them when you change trains in Chicago."

I put the tickets in my bag. John Wesley ran up and down the platform, making train noises. Pa handed me an envelope. "Here's money for food, and an extra ten dollars for emergencies," he said. "Don't lose it."

"I won't."

"Now remember, Rachel. Chicago is a big city. You mustn't talk to strangers. And when you get to

Atlanta, ask the conductor to help you find the right train to Savannah. Don't try finding it on your own."

"Don't worry, Pa. We'll be all right." I smiled at him so he wouldn't see the worry I felt at leaving him alone, with nothing but the endless, burned-out prairie to hear his thoughts. I didn't want him to know how scared I was of traveling for days through the noise and confusion of water stops and train stations, with no one to help me.

"You're a fine daughter," he said. "I depend on you much more than is fair. I hope you know I appreciate it."

I swallowed the hot tears that suddenly bubbled up.

"Don't go getting sentimental on me, now." He wiped his eyes. "It won't do for all these people to see a grown man cry."

The train chugged into the station, belching thick, eye-watering smoke, the whistle shrieking and the engine hissing. Bells clanged as the passengers got off, and others lined up to board.

Pa stood between John Wesley and me, holding our hands. "Well, I guess this is it," he said. "Have a good time with Aunt Agatha, and don't forget to mind your manners."

"We won't." John Wesley hopped impatiently from one foot to the other. "Can I get on the train now? I don't want the engineer to leave without me."

Pa chuckled and hugged him tight. "Go on, then."

John Wesley climbed aboard the train.

"Rachel."

"Yes, Pa."

"Take care of him. And yourself."

"I will. It's you I'm worried about."

"I'll be all right. This drought will be over before you know it, and we'll all be together again. You'll see."

He kissed the top of my head. "Go on, now. Find that brother of yours before he decides to drive the train himself."

Pa handed me up the steps. I found John Wesley at the back of the car and we took seats by the open window. The conductor punched our tickets, the bells clanged again, and the train began to move.

John Wesley hung his head out the window. "Bye, Pa! Take care of Jake!"

"I will, son." Pa waved his floppy brown hat as the train picked up speed. We waved till the station grew small as a toy, then disappeared as we rounded a curve.

John Wesley wiped his eyes and kicked at the seat in front of us. I stared out at the dried-up land, the only home we had ever known. Worry felt like an enormous fist in my stomach, but Pa was counting on me.

"How about a story, John Wesley?"

"Okeydoke." Snaking his arm through mine, he leaned on my shoulder. I opened our Uncle Remus book and began to read.

3

Aunt Aggie

"Hey, Rachel! There she is! That's Aunt Aggie. She looks just like Mama!" Kneeling on the train seat, John Wesley pointed to the crowd waiting on the platform.

Outside the sooty train window stood a woman who looked exactly like the picture inside my bag. Aunt Aggie was taller than Mama, but her hair was the same goldish-brown color. She wore a blue suit, shiny black boots, and a hat with a make-believe bluebird perched on top. As the train slowed, she spotted us and waved her white handkerchief.

With one last shuddering hiss, the train lurched to a halt. Wearily, I gathered my Uncle Remus book and the remains of the bread and cheese we'd bought during our stop in Atlanta. My face wore a week's worth of sweat and grime, and my clothes were wrinkled and sooty, but I was too tired to care very much. I ached from the endless journey on the hard seats, and my ears rang from the constant noise of the rails, from the wailing of babies, and the loud snoring of the two men in the seat behind me.

John Wesley looked no better. His hair was sticking up. There were bread crumbs on his shirt, and a big black smudge under one eye. His shirt and trousers were wrinkled. All in all, a sorry sight.

The minute we stepped off the train, Aunt Aggie, smelling of powder and roses, rushed over and hugged us both at once. "At last! You're finally here," she said, in a voice that made me think of honey oozing from a jar. "Now, don't move a single muscle! Stand right there and let me look at you."

She drew back and studied first me, then John Wesley. "Oh, you're Durrells all right. I can see your precious mother in both of you. And here you are, in Savannah at last. I told your father it's a pity it's taken a drought to get you down here. But no matter." She nodded, and the bluebird on her hat bobbed up and down. "What do you think of Savannah so far?"

John Wesley wrinkled his nose. "It stinks. What's that awful smell?"

Aunt Aggie laughed. "That, my dear boy, is the smell of the river. It grows on you after a while."

"I hope it doesn't grow on me! I don't want to smell like that."

"Never mind that," I said. "We must find our trunks."

Aunt Aggie put her hand on my arm. "Don't you worry about a thing, darling. Micah will take care of it."

She nodded to a tiny, white-haired man standing behind her. John Wesley followed him to the other side of the platform. Aunt Aggie adjusted her parasol and fanned her face. "I declare, this heat has been just terrible. I'm not sure your father accomplished anything by sending you here."

I looked past her, to the distant masts of the sailing boats bobbing in the river. "At least you haven't run out of water."

"Is it really that bad, Rachel?"

"Pa says he's never seen a whole year without rain. He says if it doesn't rain soon, there won't be anybody left in all of Dakota."

Micah and John Wesley came back with our trunks. "Will we be going now, Miss Durrell?" Micah asked.

Aunt Aggie's bluebird bobbed again. "By all means. The sooner we get out of this heat, the better. Come along, children."

Micah led us to a coach hitched to a team of gray horses. He lifted our trunks onto the top of the carriage and helped us inside. Then he climbed up, snapped the reins, and the horses clopped along the streets. We rolled past fine houses set behind tall black gates, past rows of pink flowers and ancient trees dripping with silvery moss. In the middle of town was a fountain with water bubbling out, and further on, rows of little iron fences that divided everything into neat squares, like our fields back home.

We rode past shops and churches, past a cemetery full of marble headstones carved with angels and lambs. As we rode along, Aunt Aggie pointed out the houses where all the important people lived. I smoothed my rumpled dress and tried to look interested, but I was hot and tired from our long trip. I wished for a cool, soft bed and a whole pitcher of water all to myself.

At last we stopped in front of a white house with round pillars and wide porches on all three floors. Behind a black iron gate, patches of pink flowers bloomed. A brick staircase curved up to the front door.

John Wesley stared first at the house, and then at our aunt. "Is this your house?"

"Indeed it is." She leaned out and pointed upward. "See that window up there? The one on the second floor, on the corner?"

We nodded.

"That was your mother's room. Mine was right next door."

"Our mother lived there?" John Wesley breathed.

"Until the day she married your daddy."

"Can we see it?" he asked, reaching for the handle on the coach door.

"In good time. Bridey's made a lovely lunch for us. It won't do to keep her waiting."

"Who's Bridey?"

Aunt Aggie gathered her gloves and parasol. "Bridey helps me keep the house running. She's been a part of this family practically forever."

"And Micah, too," John Wesley added. "He told me."

"Yes. Micah, too. He takes care of the gardens and the horses. The two of them came here from Ireland many years ago."

Micah jumped down from the driver's seat and opened the coach door, his blue eyes merry. "What about it, boyo? Wasn't that a fine ride?"

John Wesley nodded. "Can we go again to-morrow?"

"Your aunt will be deciding that one, but I don't see why not."

"You'll have plenty of time to go riding while you're here," Aunt Aggie said. "Come along now, we must find Bridey. Micah will look after the trunks."

We followed her through the gate, up the steps to the front door. It opened, and there stood a small, round woman in a flowered dress and a starched white apron. Her eyes were blue as a robin's egg and her halo of white hair stirred in the air like a dandelion.

"You look just like Micah!" John Wesley blurted. "Except you're wearin' a dress."

"John Wesley!" I poked him in the ribs. Hard. But the pink-cheeked woman laughed.

"I'm sorry," I said. "John Wesley didn't mean to be rude."

"I know that." She wiped her eyes with the corner of her apron. "We've lived together so long, Micah and I, it's hard to tell where one of us ends and the other begins. But no matter. You must be starving. Come in, the both of you, before you wilt in this heat."

Aunt Aggie dropped her things on the hall table. "Come along, children. I'll show you where to freshen up."

We followed her up a wide, curving staircase, then down a hallway with paintings of ships and horses and serious-faced ladies on the walls. The windows were open and a breeze drifted in off the river. I wanted to stand right there and cool off, but Aunt Aggie motioned me on.

"This will be your room, Rachel. And John Wesley, yours is across the hall. There's fresh water in the washstands. Hurry now. The dining room's on the first floor, at the end of the hall."

She turned away, her skirts swishing on the carpet. I looked around. The wallpaper was blue with white flowers sprinkled over it, and the bed looked like a puffy blue cloud covered with ruffles. There was a washstand, a dressing table, and a mirror in a gold frame. On the wall above the bed was a painting of an old gate open to a misty forest beyond. It was signed *S. Durrell,* the way my mother had signed all her pictures for as long as I could remember.

"Hey, Rachel," John Wesley called from the hallway. "Come and see my room."

If I'd asked John Wesley to paint a picture of the perfect place to be nine years old, it would have looked exactly like this. There was a bed and a washstand and a shelf full of books. The walls were hung with more pictures of sailing ships and steam engines, men riding horses, dogs in fields. Just beyond his window and the porch railing stood a fat-waisted oak tree, dripping moss.

"Isn't this something?" John Wesley whispered. "This was our uncle David's room, I'll bet. Remember Mama's stories about his horses? Remember when she told us about the tree house he made?"

He jerked his thumb toward the window. I knew what he was thinking. "You can't climb in the tree, John Wesley. You'll fall out and break your neck."

"I'll get a rope and tie myself in," he plotted. "I bet you can see all the way across the ocean from here."

"Nobody can see all the way across the ocean. It's too big."

"I'll make a telescope," he said. "Or maybe I'll ask Aunt Aggie to buy me one."

"You'll do no such thing! Remember what Pa said. We're not to be any trouble to her."

"But she's rich!" He waved one grimy hand in the air. "Have you ever seen such a fancy house?"

"No," I admitted. "But you aren't to ask her for things. Promise me you won't."

"Rachel? Are you coming?" Aunt Aggie called. "Bridey's waiting."

We washed up and hurried along the hall and down the stairs. "Now remember," I said. "Mind your manners."

In the dining room we sat at a round table set with pink plates, and Bridey brought platters of chicken and vegetables, plates of cakes and cookies. "Help yourselves," she said. "And don't be shy. There's more in the cupboard."

John Wesley did his best not to disappoint her. He was on his third piece of chicken when Aunt Aggie came in wearing a yellow dress with ruffles on the sleeves. She eyed the chicken bones piling up beside his plate and grinned. "Too bad you weren't hungry."

He wiped his mouth. "I'm not now. This is good."

"Well, you have Bridey to thank for that."

A wide grin split Bridey's wrinkled face. "A growin' boy needs decent food. Not that hurry-scurry train food. It's a wonder the poor lad's got enough strength left to pick up a fork."

"Indeed." Aunt Aggie's eyes met mine across the table. "I'm sorry to rush out again when you've only just arrived, but Mrs. Wentworth is giving a tea for her daughter this afternoon, and I promised to make an appearance. Olivia has been away all year, at a finishing school in Europe."

John Wesley look puzzled. "What did she look like before she was finished?" He bit into a chocolate tart.

"A finishing school is a place where young ladies go to learn the social graces," Aunt Aggie explained. "They learn to speak French and play the piano, and so on."

"Sounds boring," John Wesley said. "I'd rather be a coach driver like Micah."

"Perhaps he'll give you a few pointers while you're here. Now, I really must go. Bridey, where's my hat? The new one with the yellow feathers."

"Don't trouble yourself. I'll get it."

A moment later, we heard their voices in the hall, then the front door squeaked open and closed again. The carriage wheels rattled, and the horses' hooves rang hollow on the street.

"I'm full as a tick," John Wesley announced. "Let's go exploring."

Leaving our napkins beside our plates like Mama taught us, we hurried down the hall and nearly collided with Bridey and her laundry basket.

"Sure you nearly knocked me off my feet," she scolded. "Watch where you're goin', girl, before you hurt somebody."

"We're sorry. We finished eating," I explained.

"So I see."

"We're going exploring," John Wesley added.

"Are you now?" She hitched the basket onto her other hip. "Go along, then, but stay out of mischief."

When we reached my room, John Wesley said, "What's the matter with her?"

"Nothing. We startled her, that's all. I don't suppose she's used to having children around." Suddenly my bones felt heavy as lead. "I'm too tired to go exploring."

"I'm not! I'm going to be a detective, like Sherlock Holmes."

"Is that so? What are you planning to detect, Mr. Holmes?"

"I don't know, but there's bound to be tons of things to investigate in a big old house like this." He yawned. "I'll bet there's twenty rooms, at least."

He curled up beside me and fell fast asleep.

4

Two Letters

The days at Aunt Aggie's house passed slowly. John Wesley made a cape out of my blue shawl and tiptoed up and down the stairs. He hid behind the curtains and peeked around corners, playing detective. Aunt Aggie spent most mornings on the porch with her books, her lap desk, and a pitcher of tea. In the afternoons, she went to meetings with other ladies and came back with a determined look on her face and armloads of papers and posters.

I read my *St. Nicholas* magazines till the pages went limp. One morning I watched a wren tending her nest in an old bucket beside the gate. But mostly, I was bored. There was nobody my age for company. Aunt Aggie said most people went to the mountains in the summer, because it was cooler there. But she stayed in

Savannah because we were visiting, and because she had important work to do. I wished she would play a joke, or do something mischievous, the way she did when she and Mama were young. But she was serious as a judge, and prickly, too.

Once, I tried talking to her about Mama, and the mysterious-looking picture hanging above my bed, but she shushed me and frowned. "Gracious, Rachel. Can't you see I'm busy? Don't bother me now. And stop asking so many questions."

I hadn't felt like reading anymore, so I went to the kitchen. Bridey was there, making bread.

"What's troubling you?" she asked.

"Aunt Aggie's cross with me for interrupting her work, but honestly, Bridey, she never talks to me. She spends all her time going to stuffy old meetings and writing letters."

"Oh, she's a woman on a mission, that one is." Bridey tossed a handful of flour over the dough and gave it a sharp slap. "Won't rest till the women of the world have their equality, she says. If you ask me, that day will be a long time coming. Come over here, girl, and help me with this dough."

I brought the stool to the table and sifted on more flour while Bridey kneaded the dough. "Pa said Aunt Aggie used to be ever so much fun, playing jokes on Mama."

"She was a handful in those days, Aggie was."

"What was my mama like?"

"Well now. She was more the serious sort. Had a quiet way about her. She loved her painting, that one did. Thought nothing of going off to a party with paint beneath her nails. Your aunt Aggie scolded her about it, but it never did one bit of good that I could see."

"The picture of the old gate in my room. . ." I began.

"Arrived after your sainted mother died, from someplace in Chicago, where she'd sent it to be framed. Your poor auntie cried every time she looked at it, till one day she finally saw its meaning. Hand me that bowl, and mind you don't drop it."

"That's what I'm trying to figure out," I said. "What *does* it mean, Bridey?"

She stopped her kneading and fixed me with her robin's egg eyes. "That's for you to work out for yourself."

"Mama always said a picture should speak to a person's head and heart, not only to their eyes."

"Aye." She draped a towel over the dough and left it by the hearth to rise. "Go along now, and stay out of your auntie's way. She can be cross as a bear when she's working."

"Don't I know it! Sometimes I think she doesn't want John Wesley and me here at all."

"When I was a girl we had a saying: fish and company start to stink after three days." She laughed, but I didn't see anything funny about being unwanted and so far from home.

"Ah, child. No need for such a long face. Don't you know I'm only codding you? You're welcome as sunshine after rain."

Back in my room, I tried to read one of Mr. Twain's books, but I was homesick for Pa and Jake and Miss Burke and the prairie. I was tired of the long, hot summer. I decided to make a painting about winter in Dakota.

Most people think the prairie in winter is nothing but fields of white and gray and faded brown. But if you look closely, you can see all kinds of shapes and colors. Very early in the morning, when the winter sun first comes up, the sky is pink and gold, and the light makes the snow look blue as an ocean. In the places where the wind has blown the snow away, you can see brown tufts of broken grass sticking up like little tents, and the brittle, black stems of the dead coneflowers. If you walk outside, you can see lamplight shining gold against the crusty snow, the shadowy tracks of the coyotes and cottontails and meadow mice. Sometimes you can catch the orange flash of a hungry fox, hunting for food on the frozen earth.

I worked every morning for nearly a week to put all of it into my painting, and when it was done I signed my name in the corner, *R. Blackmon,* making my letters curly and graceful like Mama's.

"Why, this is absolutely wonderful!" Aunt Aggie said. "I hadn't realized you'd inherited your mother's talent."

"It's a gift," John Wesley said. He'd been swinging on a rope Micah tied to a tree for him, and his hair was damp against his forehead.

Aunt Aggie smiled. "Indeed. Would you mind very much if I kept this, Rachel? It will remind me of the importance of looking past the surface of things."

She carried my picture into the dining room and laid it on the table to dry, then came back and gathered her books and papers, her lap desk and tea pitcher. From across the river came the low rumble of thunder. She looked up. "Storm's brewing."

I'd been so busy with my picture I hadn't noticed that the sun had disappeared behind heavy, bruise-colored clouds.

"I don't like the looks of it," Aunt Aggie said. "We're in for a hailstorm, or worse. The last time that happened, there were so many fallen trees we couldn't get to the market for three days. We'd better stock up, just in case. Let's go find Bridey."

We found her in the kitchen, shelling peas. She looked up when we came in, but her hands kept moving, and the peas fell *plink-plink* into the bowl. "Sure, there's a storm comin', Miss Aggie. I can feel it in my bones."

"Yes." Aunt Aggie took some money from her desk drawer and handed it to Bridey. "We'll need flour and salt, and some candles, and plenty of vegetables. Get whatever looks fresh. And some strawberries, Bridey, if they have any. Rachel will help you."

Bridey set the peas on the table and took her hat from a rack beside the door. "Come on, girl."

We hurried down the walk as the clouds grew heavier and the thunder clapped and rolled.

"Hey!" John Wesley yelled from the second floor window. "Wait for me."

I turned around. The rising wind whipped my hair into my eyes. "Stay there! There's a storm coming."

"I know! You need me to protect you."

"Stay with Aunt Aggie. We'll be back soon."

Bridey laughed. "That boy is full of mischief."

She opened the gate and the wren fluttered out. We turned down the sidewalk and hurried toward the market. It was full of people talking and buying at once.

A dark-skinned girl came through the streets carrying a basket on her head. "Straw-berry!" she sang. "An' e good, an' e fine, an' e sweet, just off the vine! Straw-berry!"

Bridey handed me a sack of flour. "Careful. It's heavy."

She bought strawberries from the girl, and we finished filling our baskets. Then the sky turned black as night, and the thunder rattled the windows in the building across the street. A sudden gust of wind sent the fishmongers' baskets tumbling into the gutter. Jagged bolts of lightning split the sky.

"Run!" Bridey cried, and I ran as fast as I could, the heavy basket bumping against my legs. A coach sped past, its wheels hissing on the wet pavement. Water and mud flew onto my skirts and into my eyes.

Bridey stumbled, and her basket rolled into the street, spilling the vegetables and half a box of salt. I helped her gather the bag of flour and the peaches that had rolled into the gutter.

"That's enough!" she cried above the howl of the wind. "Come on!"

Aunt Aggie was waiting for us at the door. "Oh, dear!" She took my basket and set it on the sideboard. "I should have sent Micah with the carriage, but I didn't think the storm would move in so soon. I am sorry, darling. Run upstairs and change your clothes before you catch your death of cold."

I took off my shoes and started down the hall.

"Oh, I nearly forgot!" Aunt Aggie called after me. "A letter just came for you. From your father. It's on the table there."

A letter from Pa! My heart turned flips inside my chest. Maybe the drought had finally ended and we could go home. In my room, I hurriedly washed my face and changed into a clean dress. Then I went to find John Wesley.

He was standing with his back to the door, watching the rain lash the windows. Without turning around he asked, "Is it raining in Dakota, too?"

"I don't know," I said. "Maybe Pa mentions it in his letter."

He whirled around. "A letter?"

I held up the envelope.

"Jeepers, Rachel! Why didn't you tell me?"

"It just came. Shall I read it?"

He pretended to consider. "Oh, I don't know. Might as well. There's nothing else to do."

We sat on his bed and I opened the envelope.

"Dear Children,

I take pen in hand to tell you how very much I miss you. I am sorry to say there is no change in the weather here. Mr. Miller and I have been hauling water from the river for the animals, but we have lost a few sheep anyway and expect to lose more before it's over.

Please don't worry about me, though. I am fine, and so is Jake. He sleeps with your sock, John Wesley, every night, and sometimes, I catch him carrying it around like a favorite toy.

Speaking of toys, Miss Burke had a letter from the Walkers. It seems they are settled in Minnesota, in a place called Pipestone. Mrs. Walker said Baxter the rabbit made the trip just fine, thanks to Annie. It was kind of you, son, to give your toy to that unfortunate child. I am proud of you. And you, too, Rachel, for all you have borne with such uncomplaining grace. In spite of all that has happened to us, I am a rich man, because of you. I count the hours until we are all together again. Your loving Pa."

We sat quietly for a moment, listening to the thunder and the raindrops dancing on the roof. John Wesley stroked the letter, as if he were petting Jake. I could tell he was homesick, too. "Too bad we can't send this old Georgia rain all the way to Pa," he said. "That would fix the drought once and for all."

I put the letter back into its envelope and handed it to him. "You can be in charge of it, but don't lose it."

He brightened. "I won't. I'll put it in my secret hiding place. Come on, I'll show you."

He opened the door and peered out, like a spy on a secret mission. We tiptoed down the hall, past the parlor where Aunt Aggie sat reading, and stopped at a door that creaked when we opened it. A dark staircase led up to the attic. "Follow me," he whispered, "and watch out for the third step. It creaks, too."

At the top of the stairs we came to another door. "In here," John Wesley said. "I discovered it on my investigation."

"Does Aunt Aggie know you've been up here?" I brushed a cobweb away from my face.

"Not exactly. There's lots of good stuff up here. I bet she's forgotten all about it."

Rummaging through the musty attic, we found a gray Army uniform with brass buttons and a sword in a leather scabbard. There was a gold picture frame with one side missing and piles of dank-smelling books with red leather covers. There were wooden crates full of broken dishes, a rusty ship's bell, and a stack of crumbly newspapers with curly edges. There were two of Mama's unfinished paintings and a blue-eyed china doll with only one arm.

John Wesley put Pa's letter on a shelf above our heads where he'd already hidden his other treasures: his favorite green marble, his lucky river stone, two blue-jay feathers, and a dead butterfly. "This is my secret vault," he said. "Pa's letter will be safe here."

He led me to another dark corner. "I saved the best for last."

It was a scuffed leather trunk with a heavy lock. "I bet I can open it," he whispered.

I was curious as a cat, but I didn't feel right, snooping in Aunt Aggie's attic. "It isn't ours, John Wesley. We've no right to open it."

He shrugged and looked me straight in the eye till I gave in. "All right then. But we won't touch anything. We'll just look."

He bent over the trunk, tapped on the lock, then slapped the side of the trunk. With a sharp click, the lock sprang open. I lifted the lid.

The first thing we saw was a blue dress with a satin sash. John Wesley gripped my arm. "That's Mama's dress!"

We'd seen it a thousand times, in the picture Pa kept on the fireplace mantel. I couldn't stop staring at it.

"This must have been her trunk," John Wesley said, awe-struck. "I wonder what else is in here."

My heart was so full of grief I couldn't say a word. I stood there while John Wesley poked around and brought out a yellowed paper. "Here's a letter from Pa. I'd know his writing anywhere."

I swallowed the hard knot in my throat. "Put that back. It's hers. We shouldn't read it."

"Come on," he said. "Mama wouldn't mind."

His little face was so full of pleading and sadness that I couldn't refuse. I held the paper up to the gray light coming through the attic window.

"Dear Miss Durrell," I began.

"Who's that?" John Wesley whispered.

"Mama, of course."

"I thought her name was Blackmon, same as ours."

"It was, silly, after she married Pa. Do you want me to read this, or are you going to keep asking questions?"

"I'll be quiet. Keep reading."

"Dear Miss Durrell. I take pen in hand to thank you again for the pleasure of your company at the Summervilles' house last night. It's not often a soldier can avail himself of such pleasant company. I will be leaving on Thursday, but if you have some time before then, I would be honored to call upon you at your home. Yours truly, William Blackmon."

John Wesley frowned. "How come Pa used all those big words? He sounds like Miss Burke reading a poem. I've never heard him talk like that in my whole life."

"He was trying to impress her. So she'd see him again."

The door below us opened, and Bridey's voice echoed in the stairwell. "Hello up there! You two come to supper now, and be quick about it! Your auntie's wondering what's become of you."

John Wesley hastily plucked a small bundle from the trunk and shoved it into my hands. "Take this!"

We hurried to our rooms, and I hid the bundle under my pillow. We washed our hands and went downstairs.

The storm had passed. Micah lit the carriage lamps outside the house and the light made yellow squares in the dusk. We could smell the river and the wet earth.

There was okra stew for supper, with hot bread and butter. But I was so curious about the bundle hidden under my pillow that I could scarcely eat. As soon as we finished, John Wesley and I went back to my room and I pulled the bundle from its hiding place. A packet of letters tied with a white ribbon fell out.

"Read some more," John Wesley said, snuggling in beside me. "Read some more about Mama."

5

Aunt Aggie Makes Plans

I lit the lamp beside my bed and opened one of the letters. It made a crackling sound when I smoothed the wrinkles out.

"Dear Aggs," I began, keeping my voice low.

"Who's that?" John Wesley whispered.

"Aunt Aggie, of course. If you don't stop interrupting I won't read another word."

"I'll be still."

"Dear Aggs. The most wonderful thing has happened. William Blackmon has asked for my hand in marriage. I confess it was all so sudden, I at first hardly knew what to think. But Captain Blackmon is the kindest, most wonderful man I have ever met, and his intelligence is a pure joy to me. He knows

about art and literature and all the things dearest to my heart. And he loves to laugh."

John Wesley nodded in the near dark. "Pa loves a good joke all right."

"In short, he is the closest thing to perfection I should ever hope to find on this earth, and even though I have known him only a short time, he has won my heart."

John Wesley sat up and wrapped his arms around his knees. "What does that mean?"

"It means she loved him right away."

"Oh. What else does it say?"

"The only thing that saddens me is that he plans to leave for Dakota Territory early next year, and he wishes me to go there to make my life with him. Oh, how I shall miss Savannah, and you, dear little sister, but the prospect of living my life apart from my sweet captain is simply unthinkable."

Just then, there was a knock on my door and Aunt Aggie said, "Rachel? John Wesley? Are you in there?"

I stuffed the letters under the pillows. "Come in."

Aunt Aggie came in and sat on the chair at my dressing table. She folded her hands in her lap, like a person in church. "I've been thinking, children. It's time we discussed what to do about your schooling once the new term begins."

"School?" John Wesley sat up, plainly alarmed.

She tilted her head and her earrings sparkled in the lamplight. "The drought may go on for a long time. You may not be able to go home until spring. I promised your father I'd see to your upbringing while you're here, and that includes your education, as unappealing as it may seem."

"But we've got a school back home!" John Wesley said. "Miss Burke is a good teacher. She can catch us up in no time."

Aunt Aggie smiled. "All the same, I've made some plans. Rachel, you will attend Miss Aiken's School for Girls. Your mother and I went there."

"I bet the same teachers are still there," John Wesley said. "I bet they're about a million years old by now. They're prob'ly so moldy they creak when they walk."

"That will do, John Wesley." Aunt Aggie smiled at me. "There's an excellent art teacher at Miss Aiken's, a young woman trained in Europe. With your aptitude for painting, it would be a shame not to take advantage of the chance to study with her."

"Miss Burke teaches us art," John Wesley said. "Every Wednesday, she takes down a black book. We look at pictures and learn about appreciation."

"Learning to appreciate another artist's work is one thing," Aunt Aggie declared. "Learning to paint great pictures yourself is quite another. I won't be responsible for squandering your sister's talent."

She turned her steady gaze on him. "As for you, you will attend the Savannah Military Academy. All the Durrell men went there."

"I'm not a Durrell," John Wesley pointed out. "I'm a Blackmon."

"You're half Durrell," she said, waving one hand in the air. "You'll like the Academy. The boys wear uniforms, and practice marching, just like real soldiers."

John Wesley's eyes widened. "Uniforms? No thank you!"

"Why, John Wesley!" Aunt Aggie said. "I'm surprised. I thought you'd like the chance to become a soldier. Your grandfather fought with General Lee during the War of Northern Aggression. And your own father was a soldier for many years. It's a very honorable profession."

"I don't care!" John Wesley cried. He sent me a desperate look. "I don't want to go. Please don't make me."

Aunt Aggie frowned. "It wasn't easy to get you accepted on such short notice. I begged a favor from an old friend of your mother's. It simply won't do to refuse it now, after everyone has gone to so much trouble."

She stood up and wrapped her arms around him. "Now don't you worry about a thing. Once you've made friends, you'll like it there. I promise."

John Wesley didn't say anything. When Aunt Aggie left, he threw himself onto the bed and cried so hard I thought everybody in Savannah would hear him.

"Don't think about school yet," I said. "It won't start for two more weeks at least. Anything can happen before then. Remember how Mama fell in love with Pa practically overnight?"

He wiped his eyes with his shirtsleeve. "Read some more of Mama's letters."

But just then Bridey stuck her head in the door and crooked her finger at him. "It's way past your bedtime, boyo. But mind you don't leave your clothes lying about like you did yesterday, and don't be forgetting to wash behind your ears."

When John Wesley had scooted off my bed and trudged down the hall, she closed my door. I got ready for bed and climbed in. I thought about Pa, back home with only the bony-nosed sheep and old Jake for company. I thought about sunlight dancing on the river, the warm, milky smell of new lambs in spring, and the music of the wind in the prairie grass. I missed the whisper of Pa's scythe slipping through the weeds along the fence-rows, the smell of new hay, and the pale stars swimming in a windy sky.

My throat ached horribly. I wanted to cry. Then I remembered the money Pa had given me the day he put us on the train. It was for an emergency, but I couldn't think of anything more important than going home and saving John Wesley from being turned into a soldier against his will.

6

An Unexpected Visitor

The next day was market day and Aunt Aggie sent me to help Bridey. John Wesley was helping Micah groom the horses and Aunt Aggie was writing letters at her desk in the parlor.

I walked beside Bridey, carrying our straw baskets. Bridey wore her best blue dress and a straw hat covered with little wooden cherries that clacked when she walked.

"Bridey," I said. "You ever been anywhere on a train?"

"In the old days my sister Darby and I would take the train to Blessington to our grandmother's place. She lived in a little house at the end of a winding lane. I remember flowers blooming beside the gate, and the teakettle whistling on the black stove in the kitchen."

We stopped to let a carriage pass. Bridey said, "There was a lake not far from the house where Darby and I kept a leaky old boat. We'd sneak out at night and row across the lake and back. I still remember how pretty the moon looked, shining on the black water." She sighed. "It's all changed now, of course. Nothing ever stays the same, my girl, no matter how much we want it to."

We passed the mercantile, then the butcher shop, and the bakery where Aunt Aggie bought sweets for Sunday mornings.

"But if you *were* going somewhere," I said, "to Dakota for instance, how much would it cost?"

She stared at me. I'd made a big mistake.

"Well now. It doesn't take a genius to see what's going round in that scheming little head of yours. Sure, I can see the wheels turning. You're thinking you'll run away from your auntie's and take the boy with you."

My breath whooshed out. "We've been here almost two months. We're homesick for Pa. And John Wesley purely hates the idea of soldier school."

"The boy's a free spirit. He hates anything that keeps him from his rope swinging and horse tending. But running away only makes a problem worse." She patted my shoulder. "It's a hard truth, to be sure, but sometimes there's nothing to be done about bad times except wait for your luck to change. Sooner or later the rain will come, and your da will fetch you home again."

We turned up the street to the market and then Bridey kept me too busy to think any more about Pa or John Wesley or going home on the train. She hurried around, picking out potatoes and peaches and fish from the stalls lined up along the street. She bought sugar and salt pork and cinnamon sticks and piled everything into our baskets.

As we started home, the train whistle blew, two long, ear-splitting blasts. I thought about my emergency money, and the sad look on John Wesley's face. I had to figure out some way to get us home again, but now that Bridey knew what I was thinking, I would have to be careful.

When we got home, the front door was standing open, and Aunt Aggie was in the hallway with a man wearing a brown suit and a floppy hat. He turned around when we came up the walk. My heart stuttered. I dropped my basket and the slippery fish spilled out and went sliding down the stairs.

"Pa? Is that you?"

"Rachel!" He picked me up and whirled me around till I was laughing and crying and dizzy with relief.

"Pa, why didn't you tell me you were coming?"

He set me down and took off his hat. "I wasn't sure when I could leave, or when I would arrive. But I have a wonderful surprise for you, and I wanted to tell you in person."

Bridey bent to pick up the things that had fallen from my basket. Pa said, "Here, let me do that."

She slapped his hand away and grinned up at him. "I may be old, boyo, but I still bend. Take this other basket if you've a mind to be useful."

When we got to the kitchen, Bridey put on the kettle for tea. Pa looked around. "Where's John Wesley?"

"I sent him off with Micah," Aunt Aggie said. "He was a bit down in the mouth after our talk last night."

"I hope he's been behaving himself."

Aunt Aggie set out her blue and white cups and a plate of spice cookies sparkly with sugar. "He surprised me, William. I thought he'd be excited about attending the military school, but he was quite upset."

Pa grinned. "I'm afraid Miss Burke has spoiled him for any other school. She has a way of keeping his heart hungry for learning."

I held Pa's hand across the table. "Is the drought any better, Pa? Have we had any rain?"

"Not a drop. It's cooled off some, but we're still hauling water from the river."

The door banged open and John Wesley hurtled in. "Aunt Agatha! Guess what? Micah said—"

He stopped dead still when he saw Pa. His mouth dropped open. Then he ran to Pa and rubbed his hands all over Pa's face, feeling Pa's nose and chin and forehead like a blind person. "Holy smokes! Is it really you?"

Pa chuckled. "It's me. How are you, son?"

"Better, now that you're here. I missed you. And Jake, too. But mostly you."

Pa took John Wesley on his knee. "Well, you won't have to miss me any longer. Mr. Miller and I found another spring about ten miles downriver. And the Olsons came back two weeks ago, despite everything. Said they got to missing the land. Now that I have more men to help haul water, I won't have to be gone so long. Besides, it's just too lonesome in Dakota without you. So, drought or no drought, I've come to take you home."

John Wesley's whole face lit up. "Then I won't have to go to that school and wear a scratchy uniform, and march around all day?"

"That's about the size of it," Pa said. "Too bad for them, though. You would have made a fine soldier, John Wesley."

"I don't want to be a soldier," John Wesley said. "I want to live in Dakota."

Pa's expression grew serious. "Me, too. But we need rain."

"Pa brought us a surprise," I told John Wesley.

"What is it, Pa?" John Wesley asked. "Is it something to eat? I hope it's something to play with. I haven't had a new toy in ages."

"All in good time, son."

Curiosity drew me to the very edge of my chair, but I knew it wouldn't do any good to ask more questions. Pa would tell us when he wanted to, and nothing we could say would make it happen faster.

The kettle whistled. Bridey measured the tea leaves into the pot and poured the hot water in. Soon the kitchen smelled like sugar and cinnamon. After we had tea and cookies, Pa and Aunt Agatha went into the parlor to talk.

John Wesley followed me into my room and did a little dance. "Boy oh boy! I can't believe Pa showed up just in time." He lowered his voice. "Want to know a secret? If Pa hadn't come for us? I was going to sell my marble collection and buy a train ticket home."

"I was going to use our emergency money."

He grinned. "Oh yeah. I forgot about that. Rachel? What do you think his surprise is?"

"I don't know. Maybe he finally bought one of those new-fangled plows he's been wanting."

"Maybe, but I don't think he'd come all the way to

Savannah to tell us about it." John Wesley chewed his lip. "Maybe we're moving to Minnesota, like the Walkers."

"There's no use guessing," I said. "Pa will tell us when he's good and ready."

"Yeah. Can we read the rest of Mama's letters before we go?"

I brought them out from beneath my pillow. "There are only two more."

"Read them," he said. "Then we'll put them back in Mama's trunk."

I opened one. "She wrote this one in 1887."

"That's the year I was born!" John Wesley said, as if I didn't know. "What does she say about me?"

"Dear Aggie," I read. *"I meant to write you the news much sooner, but I've been busy. The lambs were born last month and we lost two. The others are thriving. They look so funny, leaping about on their stiff little legs. Rachel is three years old now, and into everything. But the biggest news is the birth of our own sweet lamb. John Wesley Blackmon is three months old now, and the most perfect thing you can imagine."*

"That's me!" John Wesley crowed. "She said I was perfect."

"Sometimes when I am alone here, I miss you, and Savannah, and all my friends. But when evening comes, and

the sheep are lowing in their pens, and the last of the sunlight is lying on the water, I am surrounded by the love of William and my precious babies, and I am content. It's then that I cannot imagine any other life. Give my love to Bridey and Micah. I do miss you, dear Aggie. Love, Sarah."

I folded the paper.

"Can Mama see us from Heaven?" John Wesley asked.

"I don't know."

"Will she be disappointed that I didn't go to that soldier school?"

"If Pa hadn't come for us, you would have gone, wouldn't you?"

He shrugged. "I guess. I prob'ly couldn't have got very much money for my marble collection anyway. What does the other letter say?"

Before I could open it, Aunt Aggie came in. We'd been so interested in Mama's letter, we hadn't heard her coming upstairs. She stopped in the doorway. "What are you two doing now?"

"Nothing!" John Wesley said.

"Hmmm. That usually means you're up to some mischief. What have you got there, Rachel?"

I handed her the letters. "We found them in the attic."

She sat on my bed and smoothed the pages. "I'd forgotten all about these. How long ago it all seems." Her eyes went dark with tears. "I miss her still."

"Me, too," John Wesley said. "Aunt Aggie, can we keep the letters?"

"It isn't right to go snooping through other people's things," our aunt said. "But yes, I suppose they belong with you now."

My own eyes went blurry. "Thank you, Aunt Aggie."

"You're welcome. But next time, ask my permission."

Then I thought of something else. "There's a blue dress."

"Her wedding dress," Aunt Aggie said. "She left it here for safekeeping but it's rightfully yours, too, if you want it."

"Oh, I do!"

"All right, darling. When you're ready to leave, I'll help you pack it." She kissed my cheek, and then John Wesley's. "For now, it's bedtime."

Just then, Pa came upstairs and we showed him Mama's letters.

"You can read them, too, Pa," John Wesley said. "One is about you, but I'm warning you. It's awfully mushy."

Pa's expression was sad. "Maybe another time, son. Go on to bed now."

After John Wesley had gone to his room, and Pa had turned my lamp out, I lay in the dark, wakeful as an owl, remembering the sorrowful look on Pa's face. I'd wanted him to read Mama's letters, too. But he'd hardly glanced at them.

Outside my window, a night bird trilled. I thought about when Mama died. It was in the spring, just after the lambs had been born. When our neighbors heard about Mama, they came to our farm in a long, sad caravan of wagons and buggies that stretched along the road as far as I could see. The women made a dinner and the men dug a grave on a hillside where there were trees and wildflowers.

John Wesley and Pa and I put on our best clothes. The preacher said some prayers and the men put the coffin into the hole and covered it up. The neighbors hugged me and said how sorry they were, but all their tender words couldn't solace me. Then they took their roasting pans and pie tins and went home. That was Thursday.

The next day, Pa got up before sunrise, same as usual, and made our breakfast. Miss Burke drove over in her buggy to take us to school. Then Pa went to work in our fields. It was such a wonder to me how life went right on without Mama.

At first the pain was so bad it hurt to breathe. I cried every day. Miss Burke said time would heal my wounded heart, and it was true that after a while the sharp edges of my grief began to blur, like watercolors on parchment, until one day I realized I'd gone a whole day without shedding a tear.

Pa never cried. I thought his heart must be made differently from mine, that when you were grown up, your heart couldn't break anymore. Now, I wasn't so sure. Something was bothering him, but before I could figure out what it was, I fell asleep, the last of Mama's letters still unread beneath my pillow.

7

——◆——

Pa's Surprise

Dear Agatha,

My heart is so heavy I can barely breathe. I have not been well, really, since John Wesley's birth and today the doctor gave me the news. I am dying, dear Aggie.

I know you will insist that I come home to see Dr. Tyson in Savannah, but that wouldn't change anything, even if I were strong enough to make the trip. I want to spend what time I have left with William and my precious children who will soon enough be left without a mother to care for them.

Don't let them forget how very much I loved them. Be a friend to William. Already I long for the day when we will be together again in Heaven. He is my only true love, my life, my heart. Love, Sarah

"Rachel? Hurry up! We're waiting for you!" Pa's voice drifted up the stairs. I tucked Mama's letter away and hurried downstairs.

Pa and John Wesley were in the hall with Aunt Aggie. She wore a dark green skirt and a white blouse with ruffles around the collar. She carried a straw basket with a red checked cloth on top. Pa had a blanket and some books tucked under his arm.

John Wesley bounced around as if he had springs in his legs. "Rachel! Guess what? We're going on a picnic by the river and when it gets dark we're going to see some fireworks."

Bridey handed me a straw hat like Aunt Aggie's. "You'll be needing this to keep the sun off your face."

"It's too hot." It wasn't even noon yet, but already the air was thick and still.

"Better to be hot than end up with a face like a prune," Bridey declared.

"I'll put it on when we get to the river."

"Faith, but you're a stubborn girl. Don't say I didn't warn you."

Aunt Aggie laughed, her eyes shining. "I declare, Bridey, you're fussing like a mother hen with one chick. Rachel's too young to worry about her complexion."

She patted my shoulder. "By the time you're grown up, we'll be into a whole new century. Perhaps by then women will be judged for their intelligence and compassion, and not for the number of freckles on their noses!"

"Saints above!" Pa said. "The next thing I know, you'll tell me women should have the right to vote."

Aunt Aggie's smile disappeared like the sun behind a storm cloud. "Black men have the right to vote, and it was women who helped make it happen. Surely you can see the injustice of it. The very ones who insisted that all free *men* should have a vote are denied that right for themselves. It simply isn't fair."

"It's not the same thing," Pa began. "I declare, Agatha, sometimes I—"

"Of course it's the same thing!" Aunt Aggie's chin came up. "My friends and I have been meeting every afternoon all summer, drafting a petition to the president. I'm sure *he* will see the sense of our request. I wouldn't be one bit surprised if he took it straight to the Congress himself."

Pa opened his mouth to speak, but John Wesley piped up. "Hurry up, Pa. Micah just brought the carriage around. I don't want to miss the fireworks."

Bridey snorted. "Sure, and there's fireworks a-brewing right here in this very parlor. Go along with you now, Miss Agatha, and stop all this politicky talk. No good can come of it."

Aunt Aggie tossed her head, and her knot of gold hair shone in the light. "Come along, Rachel. Perhaps you can help me change your father's mind."

Pa's brows went up, but his smile was the one he used for teasing Mama. He held the door open and we went down the steps and into the carriage.

Micah drove us through the shady streets, past gleaming white houses slumbering beneath the sun, past flower gardens and solemn churches and the long brick buildings where the planters sold their cotton before the war came. At last we came to the river and Micah stopped the carriage. Below us, the sun sparkled on the slow-moving water where boats and rafts bobbed like corks.

Pa spread our blanket beneath some trees and we feasted on Bridey's fried chicken and potato salad, and chocolate cookies, still warm from the oven. Micah stretched out in the shade and pulled his cap over his eyes. Soon we heard him snoring.

John Wesley tossed away a chicken bone and licked his fingers. "Can I go exploring, Pa?"

"Not by yourself," Pa said. "Ask Rachel to go with you."

John Wesley looked up. "Will you?"

"Wear your hat," Aunt Aggie said to me.

"I thought you said freckles didn't matter," I said.

Pa said, "Let's not get into that again!"

And they laughed together in a way that made my scalp prickle. Then it hit me. Pa and Aunt Aggie were in love. That *had* to be his surprise. Why else would he leave our farm in the middle of a drought and come all the way to Savannah?

"Come on!" I jammed my hat on, and grabbed John Wesley's hand.

He jerked away. "Don't hold my hand. I'm not a baby."

We followed a worn path along the mossy river-bank to a place where the tall trees hid us. I told John Wesley what I'd just figured out. He stared at me as if I'd suddenly sprouted another head. "Pa and Aunt Agatha? In love? You should have put that hat on a long time ago, before the sun fried your brain!"

"It's the honest truth," I said, my insides winding tight. "Didn't you see how Pa was teasing her, looking at her just the way he used to look at Mama?"

John Wesley picked up a pinecone and twirled it in his hands. "That don't mean nothin'. Pa teases everybody."

"Not like that. He's planning for her to take Mama's place. I just know it!"

"So what if it is true? Aunt Agatha's a good egg." A faraway look came into his eyes. "I wouldn't mind having a new mother, would you?"

Sometimes I missed having a mother so much I thought my heart would burst. But it didn't seem right for Pa to marry someone else when Mama was waiting for him in Heaven. The thought of it made me sick inside. I wanted to go home. I wanted things to be just the way they were before Pa sent us here, but it was a hopeless wish.

"Rachel! John Wesley!" Pa's voice echoed through the trees. "Time to go."

John Wesley said, "I'm going to ask Pa if he's going to marry Aunt Aggie."

Grabbing his collar, I pulled him around till we were standing nose to nose. "Don't you dare!"

"Why not? Don't you want to know the truth?"

"Children!" Aunt Aggie called.

We raced back to the carriage. Pa settled us inside and Micah drove us along another road, across the train tracks to a meadow beside the river. There was a bandstand with musicians playing, and people milling around, talking, and listening to the music.

We sat on our blanket. Pa went off to buy ice cream. Soon, it got dark. The music stopped and everyone clapped. Then the fireworks began.

I watched the people with their upturned faces, and the sparks exploding in the inky sky. I watched Pa and Aunt Aggie, too. They sat side by side, so close their shoulders touched. Every so often, Pa would whisper in her ear, and she would smile. Once she turned her head to look at me, but I looked away before she could catch me watching her.

A loud boom shook the riverbank. Everybody said, "Ohhh!" A rocket hissed and flared, and the sparks rained down over the dark water.

"That's the end of it," Pa said, when the crowd began to stir. "Are you still awake, John Wesley?"

"Course I am," John Wesley said. "Who could sleep through all that noise?"

Pa laughed. "You've got a point there." He picked John Wesley up and tousled his hair. "You look tired, though. It's been a long day."

"But a very nice one," Aunt Aggie said. "Even if we didn't always agree."

We gathered our things and started home. It was the middle of the night and only a few lights glimmered in the dark streets. The carriage rocked like a cradle and the horses' hooves echoed on the pavement. I was nearly asleep when Pa said quietly, "Children?"

John Wesley yawned and rubbed his eyes. "What is it?"

"Remember the surprise I promised you?"

I sat up, my heart jumping in my chest like popcorn in a hot skillet.

"We already guessed!" John Wesley blurted. "You're going to marry Aunt Agatha."

Aunt Aggie let out a whoop. "Mercy sakes! Where did you get a notion like that?"

Pa laughed, too. "Your aunt is one fine woman, but we're different as night and day."

Aunt Aggie said, "Your daddy is just about the best friend I ever had, even if we haven't seen each other very often. But I wouldn't last a month in Dakota. It's too cold, and too far away from everything I love."

I leaned against the carriage seat, weak with relief. I didn't want Pa to marry anybody. He belonged to Mama and she belonged to him. Forever.

"Then what's the surprise?" John Wesley asked.

Micah turned the carriage into the drive. The front door opened and Bridey peered out.

"You're partly right," Pa said to John Wesley. "I have decided to marry again. But not your Aunt Agatha."

"Then who is it, Pa? Who's going to be our new mother?"

"Miss Burke," Pa said.

8

Aunt Aggie's Promise

I couldn't believe it. Pa and our teacher? It was as if everything I knew to be solid in the world suddenly melted into thin air. My eyes went blurry. I couldn't breathe. Micah opened the carriage door and I tumbled out and raced up the steps to the front door.

Bridey cried, "What is it, girl? You're running as if the devil himself is after you."

I didn't answer her. I ran upstairs to my room and slammed the door. I slammed it hard. I hoped the whole house would fall down.

"Rachel, honey," Pa said, from the other side of the door.

"Leave me alone! I don't want to talk to you."

"Hey Rachel, it's me," John Wesley said. "Let me in."

"Go away."

He came in anyway, and sat on the edge of my bed. "For gosh sakes, Rachel. Don't cry. You'll make me cry, too."

I sat up. "How could Pa do this to her?"

"Who? Miss Burke?"

"No, you little goose! Mama! How could he marry somebody else, after what Mama said about him? After she said he was her heart, and her whole life, and she would wait for him in Heaven?"

"Maybe she's been gone so long he forgot." John Wesley propped his head on my pillow. "Sometimes I forget, too. And it makes me scared when I can't even remember the color of Mama's eyes. I don't want to forget her. But sometimes I can't help it."

"You were so little when she died," I said.

"I remember how she and Pa used to dance, though. Pa would twirl her around and she would laugh and laugh. Even when there wasn't any music."

"She loved to dance."

"Will Miss Burke dance with Pa?"

"I don't know. I don't want to think about her."

"I thought you liked her."

"Not anymore, I don't."

"It might not be so bad," John Wesley said. "If she's our new mother, maybe she won't make me do any more arithmetic. Maybe she won't count off when I spell a word wrong, or keep me from recess just 'cause I'm five minutes late."

"How can you be so selfish? All you can think about is what's in it for you!"

He sat up. "You're the one who's selfish. Didn't you see how shiny Pa's eyes got when he talked about marrying her?"

I wanted to tell him he was a hundred percent wrong, but I *had* seen the pure happiness in Pa's eyes. All the same, I didn't see how Miss Burke ever could belong in our family. We already had a mother, even if we couldn't see her anymore. Nobody could ever take her place. That was the open and shut truth of it.

"Rachel? John Wesley?" It was Pa again. "Time for bed. We're going home tomorrow and we all need our rest."

John Wesley slid off my bed. "Don't cry anymore. It'll be all right. You'll see."

He left me alone in the warm dark. I tried to sleep, but I couldn't. I kept thinking about Mama. How could Pa marry someone else? It was as if he'd painted Mama right out of our lives, as if she'd never even existed. As if she never mattered at all.

Right then, I made myself a promise. I couldn't stop Pa from marrying Miss Burke, but I would never go back to her stupid school. And I would never speak to her again. Not in one million years.

The next thing I knew, it was morning and the house smelled like maple syrup. I was getting dressed when Aunt Aggie came in carrying a white bundle. "Here's your mother's dress. I wrapped it in muslin so it won't get dirty on the trip home."

My throat swelled with tears. "I don't want it."

"Of course you do. You're upset, that's all. This news has taken us all by surprise." She smoothed the blue coverlet on my bed. "I'll tell you something, Rachel. I tried not to show it, but I was angry when your father announced his plans last night. It breaks my heart to think of anyone taking Sarah's place in his affections, but now that I've thought about it, I suppose it's unfair to expect him to go on alone forever."

"He isn't alone! He has me, and John Wesley and Jake, and all our friends."

"It isn't the same thing. In time you'll see that. And after a while, you'll get used to the idea."

"I don't want to get used to it. Why does Pa want to change everything? Our life is fine just the way it is."

"I know how you feel." Aunt Aggie put her arms around my shoulders. "But the truth is, we can't undo the past. And the future arrives whether we want it to or not." She tipped my chin up till our eyes met. "We must learn to bend, dear, or life will break us. Give this Miss Burke a chance. She just might make a fine mother."

"She's my *teacher!* She can't take Mama's place."

"Of course not. But perhaps you and John Wesley can make a new place for her. It's worth thinking about."

Opening my trunk, she carefully placed Mama's dress inside. "Come along now. Bridey will skin us both if we let her pancakes get cold."

We went down to breakfast. Pa smiled at me when I slid into my chair. I ignored him and stared at my plate. I didn't feel like eating a single bite, but Pa's surprise hadn't affected John Wesley's appetite one bit. He ate two stacks of pancakes with extra syrup, and three pieces of bacon, too.

After breakfast, it was time to go. Micah brought the carriage around and helped Pa load our trunks. Bridey hugged me so hard my breath sighed out. "Be a good girl, Rachel, and don't be giving your da any more grief. Lord knows the poor man's had more than his share already."

"Hey, Bridey," John Wesley said. "You want to keep this green marble, so you won't forget me?"

She laughed. "I won't be forgetting you, but thank you. That marble will look handsome on my kitchen shelf."

Aunt Aggie pinned on her yellow hat and came with us to the train station. Pa bought our tickets and the stationmaster took our trunks.

"I wish you were coming out for the wedding, Agatha," Pa said. The whistle blew, and people began boarding the train.

"I'll come out next spring," she said, above the *chuff-chuff* of the engine, "after everything is settled." Standing on tiptoe, she kissed Pa's cheek. "Be happy, William."

I couldn't believe it. Just this morning, she'd told me how angry she had been at Pa for promising to marry Miss Burke. Now she was acting as if it was perfectly fine for Pa to take another wife. It was plain neither of them loved Mama. Not really.

I turned away and started up the steps to the train. Pa pulled me back. "Aren't you going to say good-bye to your aunt?"

"Good-bye," I said.

"Bye-bye, darling. Thank you for the beautiful painting." Aunt Aggie put her hands on my shoulders. "Next year I'll take you to New York, to see the paintings at the Metropolitan. We'll stay in a hotel and go to the theater. We'll have a lovely time, you'll see."

Then she pulled me close and whispered in my ear, so Pa couldn't hear. "You're confused just now, but someday, you will understand. That's a solemn promise."

John Wesley said, "Bye, Aunt Agatha. I had fun, except for worrying about that soldier school."

She laughed and kissed his cheek. "Bye, John Wesley. If you change your mind someday, come back and I'll see if they'll let you in."

He saluted and climbed onto the train. We took our seats by the window. Pa sat facing us. The whistle blew again and the train started to move.

Aunt Aggie called out, "Good-bye! Write to me, Rachel!" and waved her handkerchief till we couldn't see her anymore.

John Wesley settled into his seat. "How long till we're home, Pa?"

"If we don't have any delays, we'll be home by Friday."

"Good-o." John Wesley grinned. "I want to see Jake. I've missed him something awful."

"He missed you, too," Pa said. "But not as much as I did. It got mighty lonely out there at night with nothing but the wind for company."

"Pa," John Wesley said. "After Miss Burke is our mother, will she still be our teacher?"

"I'm afraid not, son. Only unmarried ladies can be teachers. It's a rule."

"What will she do all day?"

"Oh, I imagine she'll stay busy. There's always plenty to do around our place."

I looked out the train window at the land and houses flowing past, and thought about all the work of running our farm. There was planting, plowing, and hoeing the fields, and spring lambs to be birthed. There were cows to milk, chickens to feed, eggs to gather. In the summer there were vegetables to be picked and preserved for the winter, and sheep to shear. There were floors to scrub and quilts to make, and fences to mend. In the winter, when the snow lay knee-deep in the fields and the river froze to solid ice, there was firewood to be hauled to the hearth from the woodpile out back.

And then I realized something. Miss Burke knew practically everything about history and literature, art and music. She could make beautiful curly letters on the chalkboard and play songs on the piano without missing a single note. She could recite entire poems by heart.

But she had never stood ankle-deep in mud in the middle of a wet spring night, pulling a slippery lamb from its mother. She had never hammered a fence or milked a cow or fought a prairie fire.

Once she saw how hard it was, she would go far away from Dakota and find another place to teach school. Pa might be sad for a little while, but he would get over it soon enough, just the way he'd gotten over Mama.

And then life would go back to the way it was supposed to be. I felt so much better that when Pa smiled at me, I actually smiled back. As the train picked up speed, I settled into my seat, feeling ever so much better. Things just might work out after all.

9

Home Again

Mr. Miller and Jake came in a wagon to meet us at the train station. Jake whimpered and barked and licked our faces. John Wesley wrestled him to the ground and tickled his belly, and his legs wiggled in the air.

"He's glad to see us, Pa!" John Wesley said happily. He kissed Jake's huge old head. "I missed you, boy!"

Mr. Miller shook Pa's hand. "Glad you made it back, William. It's sure been lonesome around here since the Andersons left."

"The Andersons have gone, too?"

Mr. Miller nodded. "Last week, headed for Illinois. Besides us and the Olsons and the Ludke brothers, this part of the state is nearly deserted."

"It hardly seems possible," Pa said. "Seems like it was only yesterday that people were pouring in here by the hundreds."

"That was before this drought," Mr. Miller said. "The best land in the world won't do you any good if it never rains. I guess you can't blame folks for cutting their losses and moving on."

John Wesley looked up. "Did Miss Burke move, too?"

For a moment, my hopes soared, but Mr. Miller said, "No, but if we don't get more families moving back, there won't be any need for the school."

He took off his hat and wiped his forehead. "She does a lot for folks around here."

That much was true. Miss Burke wrote up stories for the newspaper in Yankton. She organized dances for the grown-ups and planned summer picnics by the river. She was in charge of the Christmas program, too. It would be hard to do without her, but not as hard as sharing my pa with her.

Just then a black buggy rattled down the road and stopped right in front of us. Miss Burke got out and ran to Pa, laughing, her wide, gray eyes full of light. "William! I thought you'd never get here!"

Pa took her hand. "Hello, Grace. I'm glad to be home."

She smiled up at him. "I missed you something awful."

I thought I was going to be sick.

Miss Burke smiled at John Wesley and me. Then she said to Pa, "Have you told them?"

He nodded. "It's been a bit of a shock, I'm afraid."

She said to me, "I know it seems sudden, but I've admired your father for a very long time. It was a pure joy to me to discover he returned my tender feelings. And you and John Wesley and I get on so well at school I feel I'm practically a part of your family already."

My eyes burned. I had to bite my tongue to keep from shouting that she most certainly was not part of our family, and never would be, no matter what.

Mr. Miller said, "William? Are these all of your trunks?"

Pa glanced at the wagon. "I think so. Come on, children. Round up that dog and let's go home."

I climbed onto the wagon with John Wesley. We sat facing backward, with our legs hanging off the back. Jake squeezed in between us, a dumb dog-grin on his face. Pa said something to Miss Burke and helped her back into her buggy. She gave Pa a basket covered with a white cloth, and we started home.

Miss Burke followed behind our wagon until we reached the fork in the road. "Bye, children!" she sang. "I'll come see you tomorrow!"

"Don't bother," I muttered.

"Bye, Miss Burke!" John Wesley stood up in the wagon and waved to her. She waved back.

I was furious with him. "What did you do that for? You'll only encourage her."

"Pa's already made up his mind. There's nothing we can do about it."

"Maybe not, but we don't have to pretend to like it."

He squinted up at me. "Are you gonna be grumpy forever?"

"Maybe."

He wrapped his arms around Jake's shaggy neck. "I liked you better when you weren't cross all the time."

"Well you can thank Miss Burke for that! It's her fault."

The wagon bumped over the rutted road. We creaked up a hill and then down again, and there was our farm, shining in the white-hot sun. Mr. Miller halted the wagon in the front yard. Jake jumped out and turned in circles, barking and nipping at my skirts.

Mr. Miller helped Pa carry in our trunks. "Olson

and I hauled water for the stock this morning, and filled up the crocks in the kitchen," he said. "You should have enough for a couple of days if you're careful." He eyed Miss Burke's basket. "Ellen sent you some supper, but I see Grace Burke is already taking care of you."

"I can't thank you enough," Pa said. "You've been a good neighbor."

"You'd do the same for me," Mr. Miller said.

We followed him into the yard. Mr. Miller climbed on to his wagon. Pa said, "You and your missus will come for the wedding, won't you?"

"I wouldn't miss the chance to see you all trussed up like a Thanksgiving turkey," Mr. Miller teased. "And Ellen's talked of nothing else all week. The way she's carrying on, you'd think she was the one gettin' married."

"Grace and I will try to make it a worthy occasion."

Grace and I! It was so disgusting I almost gagged.

John Wesley came out, his cheeks puffed out like a chipmunk's. He swallowed. "Hey, Pa. You should try some of Miss Burke's cake. It's delicious."

Mr. Miller picked up his reins. "See you next Saturday, William. Unless you get a bad case of cold feet."

John Wesley licked the icing off his fingers. "Cold feet? Your shoes got holes in 'em, Pa?"

Pa grinned. "Mr. Miller means I might suddenly get scared about getting married again."

I scarcely heard them. Next Saturday, Mr. Miller said. That meant I had only a week to show Miss Burke she was not cut out to live on our farm and be our mother. Not by a long shot.

Mr. Miller's wagon rattled out of the yard. After supper, while Pa and John Wesley tended the sheep, I unpacked my trunk. Then I took paper and a pen from Pa's shelf and sat down at the table. Dipping the pen into the inkwell, I began to write.

10

A Perfect Plan

When Miss Burke arrived the next day, I was ready for her. I'd made a list of onerous chores guaranteed to make her leave us for good. The list said:

Feed the sheep and clean out their pens. It was too bad there were no lambs waiting to be born. That would have been even messier, but it was September now. There wouldn't be any more lambs till spring.

Mend stockings. My sewing basket was full of socks with holes in the toes. Once Miss Burke poked a thousand holes in her fingers with the darning needle, she'd think twice about marrying Pa.

Kill a chicken for supper. Even I had never done this. It was too awful. I always made Pa do it. I was certain Miss Burke couldn't do it either. Once she'd tried all those chores, she'd see she didn't belong on our farm.

It was a perfect plan.

Miss Burke tied her horse in the shade and stepped onto the porch. "Good morning, Rachel. Is your father here?"

"He and John Wesley went to get more water."

"Oh." She looked so disappointed I nearly felt sorry for her. Then she said, "Well, this is better actually. We'll have a chance to visit without the men around."

She was trying to win me over, but I didn't want to be won. "I don't have time for visiting," I said. "I'm the woman of this house. I have chores to do."

"I'll be glad to help," Miss Burke said. "We can talk all the while and then the work won't seem so unpleasant. What should we do first?"

I showed her out to the sheep pens and handed her Pa's shovel. "We have to muck out the pens, put down fresh straw, and throw in some feed."

"Oh, is that all?" Without another word, she tucked up her skirts, picked up the shovel and waded into the stinking muck. "I'll start on this side, and you can start over there. This won't take any time at all."

As we started shoveling, Miss Burke said, "Tell me about Savannah. I've heard it's a beautiful city."

"It's all right. I like Dakota better."

She pitched a shovelful of sheep droppings over the fence. "I don't blame you. I like it here myself."

I frowned. Why did she have to be so agreeable?

"I imagine your aunt Agatha was happy to see you," Miss Burke said.

"I suppose."

"Did you have a good time?"

"It was all right."

We shoveled for a while without talking. Finally, Miss Burke tossed one last shovelful over the fence and straightened. "There! All finished. Where's the pitchfork? I'll get the hay."

I was too worried to do more than point the way to the barn. Running her off might be harder than I'd planned.

In a minute she was back with a wheelbarrow full of hay. Taking up the pitchfork, she tossed the hay over the fence as if it were light as a feather. When that was finished, she wiped the sweat off her brow and dusted her hands together. "There! I'm sure the sheep will appreciate having clean pens. But let's let John Wesley put out the feed when he returns. I could use something to drink."

Before I knew what was happening, she marched back to the kitchen and made lemonade. She poured the water carefully so as not to spill a drop. She rolled the lemons and sliced them with Mama's kitchen knife, then measured out the sugar and stirred it into the crock. She poured two glasses and handed me one.

It was delicious. Not too sweet and not too sour. Just the way Pa liked it. Miss Burke tucked a strand of hair behind her ear. "What's next?"

"Socks," I said. "They need darning."

"Lead the way."

In the parlor, I took down my basket, the darning needles, and the smooth wooden darning egg that had been Mama's.

"This brings back wonderful memories," Miss Burke said, turning the egg over in her hand. "When I was a girl, my mama and I darned socks every Saturday."

I went on sorting John Wesley's socks from Pa's longer ones.

"I had seven brothers, you see, so there were always plenty of socks with holes in the toes." She paused for a minute. "How do you suppose they manage to wear them out so quickly?"

I shrugged.

Taking up one of Pa's brown socks, she said, "Heavens! You can see where his big toe poked right through. Well, hand me the needle, Rachel. This won't take a minute."

She worked the darning egg into Pa's sock and picked up the needle. It went in and out very fast, clicking against the wooden egg inside. She didn't prick her fingers with the needle. Not once. I tried to see exactly how she did it. After I had run her off, I would have to mend the socks. It would be good not to end up with sore fingers again.

The pile of socks got smaller and smaller until they were all mended and folded neatly in my basket. "There!" Miss Burke said. "That didn't take long."

We heard the wagon rumbling down the road. She stood up and smoothed her hair. "That must be your father!"

The wagon rattled up the rise and into the yard.

"Whoa!" Pa pulled on the reins and the wagon creaked.

He and John Wesley and Jake jumped off. Pa took off his hat and wiped his forehead. "Hotter than blazes again today. I don't know how much longer we can go on."

Miss Burke put her hand on Pa's sleeve. "Try not to worry. Surely the rain will come soon."

"It has to," Pa said. "We lost four more sheep last night. And that new spring we found is running low. We've been rationing their water, and there's only so much those poor creatures can take."

Then he smiled at Miss Burke. "But there's no need to burden you with all this. Have you had a good visit with Rachel?"

"We've been busy with chores," Miss Burke said. "But Rachel is excellent company, just as she is at school."

John Wesley said, "Pa says you won't be our teacher anymore after you get married."

"That's right. But I can still help you with your studies. Who knows? You might finally learn those multiplication tables."

"Multiplication?" He whirled around and whistled for Jake. "Come on, boy. Let's get out of here."

Pa shook his head. "I hope you know what you're getting into, Grace. That boy has a heart bigger than Texas, but he can be a handful."

"You're forgetting I grew up in a house full of older brothers," she said, smiling. "I think I can handle one small boy."

"Rachel," Pa said. "Would you bring some water? I want to speak to Miss Burke for a minute."

There. It was already starting. They weren't even married yet, and already she was taking Pa away from me. I stomped up the steps.

Miss Burke called, "Rachel? Bring your father some of that lemonade instead." To Pa she said, "We just made it."

"Lemonade!" Pa said. "You're spoiling me."

"I enjoy spoiling you, William."

They gave each other a long, sappy look that made my stomach lurch.

I poured them some lemonade and went around to the back porch. The hens were clucking and scratching in the dirt. Then I remembered the last chore on my list and I felt better. Anybody could shovel sheep droppings or mend a sock, but it took real guts to kill a chicken. Miss Burke could never do it. Then she would see she didn't belong here.

Pa came around back and stood with me in the yard, his empty glass in his hand. "Miss Burke is trying very hard to be mindful of your feelings," he said. "It would please me greatly if you'd respect hers."

"I've been polite!"

"Maybe so, but her shoes are filthy. Looks to me like you sent her to muck out the sheep pens."

"She wanted to do it! She said chores go faster when you have company."

"All the same, I won't have you treating her like a servant."

"I suppose it's all right for her to treat me like one, though!"

"I never said that. And she's not treating you unfairly. If anything, she's been way too lenient with you this morning. You know what I mean, Rachel. I'll have no more talk about it."

Handing me his glass he said, "I'm taking John Wesley into town to help load the feed. We'll be back for supper. And I expect to see your attitude much improved by then. Do you understand?"

"Yes, Pa."

"That's my girl. Now go find Miss Burke. It isn't polite to leave a guest alone."

I went inside. Miss Burke was standing at the fireplace mantel, looking at Mama's picture. "Your mother was very beautiful, Rachel. And I can already see, you're going to look just like her when you grow up."

"You don't have to be nice to me," I said.

"I'm not being nice. I truly mean it. You have the same lovely eyes, the same nose, and cheekbones."

To my horror, my tears leaked out, and rolled down my cheeks. Miss Burke tried to hug me but I backed away.

She twisted her hands, "I *am* sorry, Rachel. I never meant to make you cry."

"I don't care what you meant!" I shouted. "Why won't you go away and leave us alone? Can't you see you're not wanted here?"

"Oh!" Her eyes went shiny, and her voice wobbled. "You selfish, inconsiderate girl!"

"Grace?" Pa's voice boomed out. "John Wesley and I are leaving now. Do you need anything from town?"

She took a deep shuddering breath and made her voice shiny-bright. "Not a thing! Thank you anyway."

The wagon rolled out of the yard. It seemed that we stood there forever, staring at each other across the parlor. Finally, Miss Burke said, "Forgive me. I didn't mean a word of that."

I clenched my fists and stared out the window, listening to the hot wind shivering the browned-out grasses.

Miss Burke sighed. "We always got on so well at school, I never dreamed this would be so difficult. For your father's sake, Rachel, I want us to get along. May we forget what just happened, and start over again?"

I didn't feel like forgetting. I wanted to hold on to my anger till she climbed back in her buggy and drove away for good. But it was plain she wasn't going anywhere, at least not right away.

I pasted on my smile, like a person in a play. "Let's make fried chicken for supper. It's Pa's favorite."

Miss Burke pasted on her smile, too. "That's a fine idea. Why don't you pick out a good one and dispatch the poor thing while I get the potatoes ready?"

"Me?" I swallowed hard. My perfect plan was turning out all wrong.

She glanced at the clock on the mantel. "If we hurry, we'll have time to bake a pie, too. You can pluck the chicken while I make the crust." She twirled around and clapped her hands, as if she'd truly forgotten our hateful words. "We'll make this our first family dinner."

And our last, if my plan worked.

"Miss Burke?"

She was bustling around rattling pots, taking out Mama's roasting pan and pie tins as if my kitchen and everything in it already belonged to her. "Yes?"

"I can't, um, dispatch the chicken."

"Why ever not?"

"It's the feather dust. It gets in my lungs and I can barely breathe. Once I nearly died. But Mama saved me."

"Goodness! I had no idea. When was this, Rachel?"

"Oh, a long time ago. It's an affliction I've had all my life. So Mama always killed the chickens. Or Pa. I can't do it. It's not safe."

She chewed her lip. "No, I suppose not. Can you at least help me chase one down?"

"I guess it wouldn't hurt, as long as I don't breathe too much feather dust."

"Very well. Let's get it over with."

We went outside and chose a fat white hen taking a dust bath in the shade. "Go around behind her," Miss Burke whispered, "and shoo her this way. I'll grab her when she comes by."

I sneaked up behind the chicken and started her toward Miss Burke, but the chicken seemed to know what was happening. She cocked her eye and gave me a baleful stare, then flapped under the porch. Miss Burke handed me the shovel and squatted at the other end of the porch. "Use this to drive her out."

With the shovel handle, I poked the chicken. It squawked and flapped itself right into Miss Burke's arms.

Miss Burke flinched and blinked her eyes, but she didn't let go of the chicken even when it clawed her hands. She said, "I'll tell you something, Rachel. I've done a lot of things in my time, but I have never once murdered a chicken. Tell me, how does one do it, exactly?"

I started to tell her how Pa wrings their necks. One quick twist of his wrist and the chicken flops onto the ground and dies. But that seemed too quick and clean, too easy. Not a real test of how much Miss Burke wanted into my family.

Pa's ax was sticking in the stump by the woodpile, the top of the blade shining in the sun.

"You see that stump over there?" I pointed to the ax.

Still clutching the squirming chicken against her chest, she nodded and swallowed hard.

"Well, Pa puts the chicken on the block and chops its head off with the ax."

She shuddered. "I see. We'd best get on with it then."

"Oh, I dare not go any closer. Feather dust."

She squared her shoulders and carried the chicken to the chopping block, her skirts trailing in the dust. With one hand she held the chicken down. With the other, she jerked the ax out of the stump. Then she turned her head and looked at me across the empty yard, and I saw that she understood everything.

The sun burned my eyes. The air was thick and still. Far off, I heard the bleating of sheep and the faint tinkling of their bells. The look in her eyes filled me with shame, but somehow, I couldn't stop the awful test I'd set for her.

The ax rose and fell, and the chicken squawked. She screamed as blood sprayed the stump, the ax, the starched bodice of her dress. I felt dizzy. I hadn't known chickens bled so much.

Then I saw it wasn't the chicken's blood spreading out in a dark, rust-red stain. It was her own.

11

—·—

Grace

Miss Burke sank to her knees in the dirt.

I couldn't move or think. I could only stare at her through the thick, shimmery heat.

"Rachel! Help me!"

The ax had made an ugly gash in her arm. Her lips turned blue. Her eyes were wide and staring. Blood spilled out and dripped into the dust.

"Rachel. You must stop the bleeding." She didn't sound like Miss Burke at all. She sounded like a little girl, her voice high and squeaky.

"What should I do?" I cried.

She fainted, and lay crumpled on the ground like a broken doll. Panic rose up inside my chest as I realized there was no one to help me. Her horse and buggy were tied in the front yard, but it would take too long to drive all the way into town and back. I couldn't leave her lying there, bleeding into the hard, cracked earth.

I ran to the house for Pa's tin of yellow salve and a clean rag for making a bandage. I smeared on some salve, and wrapped the bandage tighter and tighter around her arm, till her hand puffed up like a bee sting. Then I brought water from the crock in the kitchen and poured it over her face till she sputtered and opened her eyes.

"Help me inside," she said weakly.

I helped her to her feet and put my arm around her waist. We crossed the yard and went up the steps and into the house. In the parlor, I eased her onto the settee, then brought her some lemonade.

"Miss Burke?" I was trembling like an old ewe at shearing time. "Does it hurt very much?"

"Not yet," she said. "But I suppose it will later."

She loosened the bandage and moved her fingers. "At least the bleeding has slowed. You were right to wrap it so tightly."

I felt horrible. "I'm sorry!" I said. "I never meant for this to happen."

"I know. Go get supper started. And make some tea, if you don't mind."

When the fire got going, I put the kettle on, my thoughts tumbling and bubbling like boiling water. I was scared of what Pa would say when Miss Burke told him how I'd tricked her with my lies about the feather dust. I worried about what would happen if she got sick and died.

The clock struck five. Pa and John Wesley would be home soon. I peeled potatoes, which took nearly forever, because my hands were shaking so. I set them on to boil, sliced some bread, and put out the last of the food Mrs. Miller had sent. When the tea was ready, I took some to Miss Burke.

Soon we heard the wagon rumbling along the road, and the jangle of the harness, and then Pa's voice booming out, "Whoa, there!"

John Wesley burst through the door, a brown bundle tucked under his arm. "Look, Miss Burke! New clothes! For the wed—holy Moses! What happened to your arm?"

"Where's your father?" Miss Burke sat up and pushed her hair off her face.

"Unhitching the team," John Wesley said. "But Miss Burke, you're hurt."

Pa came up the steps and pushed open the door. "Rachel? Grace?"

"In here, William!" Miss Burke called.

I stayed in the kitchen, stirring the potatoes, till Pa took my hand and led me across the hall to the parlor. Behind his dusty spectacles, his eyes were twinkling the way they did when he had a wonderful secret he was dying to share. I couldn't remember the last time I'd seen him so happy. And I had spoiled everything. I felt empty, as if a raging prairie fire had turned my insides to ashes.

"Grace?" Pa dropped my hand the moment he saw Miss Burke lying on the settee. "Merciful Lord! What happened to you?"

The whole house went quiet as a tomb, as if something had sucked out all the sound. I held my breath. Now Miss Burke would tell Pa everything. He would never forgive me. And the love I was trying so hard to hold on to would disappear forever.

"It was an accident." Miss Burke's eyes, sad and gray as an unsettled sky, were steady on mine. "Rachel and I decided to make fried chicken for supper, but I'm afraid neither of us had any idea about how to kill the poor thing. The ax slipped."

"Merciful Lord!" Pa said again. "You stay right there. I'll get the doctor."

"Really, William, there's no need. It's only a flesh wound. Rachel took good care of me. I'll be all right."

That was all. Not a word about the odious chores I'd heaped on her shoulders all day. Not a word about how I'd practically dared her to kill the chicken with the ax. Not a word about feather dust.

The potatoes boiled over on the stove, hissing and steaming. I went to the kitchen and lifted the pot off the fire. I stirred in the salt and butter, and put them into a bowl. John Wesley came in and poured milk into our glasses.

We set out our plates, listening to Pa and Miss Burke talking low in the room across the hall. The murmur of their voices was a sweet sound that reminded me of how things used to be, when Mama was alive.

Miss Burke gave a quiet little laugh, and Pa laughed, too. Maybe Aunt Aggie was right. Maybe Pa needed somebody his own age to talk to. Somebody to fill up the empty place in his heart that got put there when Mama left us. It was a kind of emptiness that John Wesley and I just couldn't fill up, no matter how hard we tried. It felt strange to think of another woman in my mother's house, but it was plain Miss Burke loved Pa too much to be discouraged by the hardships of life on the prairie. She would stay.

I could never call her Mama, but I couldn't very well call her Miss Burke, either. Besides, once she married Pa, she wouldn't be Miss Burke anymore. I said her name under my breath, trying it out. "Grace."

John Wesley lit the lamps. Pa put his arm around Miss Burke and helped her to Mama's chair at the table. After the blessing, he spooned her food onto her plate. He even buttered her bread for her. John Wesley grinned when he saw that.

"Miss Burke will stay here tonight," Pa announced. "I'll take her home in the morning."

"Where will she sleep?" John Wesley slipped Jake a bite of bread, and the old dog's tail thumped on the floor.

"She can have my bed and I'll bunk with you. All right?"

John Wesley nodded happily. "We can pretend we're Lewis and Clark, camping on the Missouri."

After supper, Pa and Miss Burke sat on the porch talking, while John Wesley and I washed and dried the dishes.

"Were you scared when Miss Burke got hurt?" John Wesley's plate squeaked against the dish towel.

"I didn't know what to do. It happened so fast."

"Why didn't she just wring that chicken's neck, like Pa does?"

"I don't know."

"Didn't you tell her how Pa does it? How come you let her pick up that ax in the first place?"

"I don't know! Hand me that bowl and stop asking so many questions."

We finished the dishes and Pa and Miss Burke came inside. Pa read to us till it was time for bed. I helped Miss Burke unfasten her dress. She sighed. "I always liked that dress, but I suppose now it's only good for the rag bin."

She pulled the pins from her hair and combed through it with her fingers. I couldn't stop staring at the bloody, crusty bandage on her arm. She looked up, and I thought she was going to talk about what had happened in the yard, but all she said was, "Would you bring me some water?"

I poured some from the crock and set it by the bed. She got into bed and I folded back the covers.

"Miss Burke?"

"Good night, Rachel. I'm too tired to talk now."

A vast, cold silence settled between us. There was nothing to say. I crossed the hall to my room.

Pa was still up. The lamps in the parlor were out, but I could hear the *squeak-squeak* of his rocking chair on the porch. I got ready for bed and turned out my lamp.

After a while I heard Pa climb the ladder to the loft where John Wesley slept, and then their voices, soft in the dark. Outside, Jake whined and went back to sleep under the porch.

My window was open, but the house was hot as an oven. I turned over, looking for a cooler spot on the sheets. Then came a low rumble, like the sound of a wagon on the road, but I couldn't imagine who would be traveling so late at night. The sound came again, and I sat up in the dark. Thunder!

Hoping for rain, I tiptoed out to the porch, my heart beating hard and fast. I searched for clouds, but there weren't any. A million stars swam in the clear, hot sky. A sudden flash lit the darkness, and I saw Miss Burke sitting on the porch, watching me.

She motioned me to sit beside her. "I couldn't sleep either."

I sat down, but I didn't know what to say. I hated the uneasiness that lay between us, and the shameful feelings pushing against my heart. "I wish it would rain."

"Mmmm." Miss Burke drew her sheet about her shoulders.

"I'm sorry for everything," I said. "For making you shovel the sheep pens, and darn the socks, and kill the chicken. And I didn't mean those awful things I said."

"I know. You're made of finer stuff than that."

"I'm glad you didn't tell Pa."

"I did it more for his sake than yours."

All at once, I started to cry, great heaving sobs that nearly stole my breath. The thunder rumbled again. Jake scrambled from beneath the porch and laid his head in my lap. I buried my tear-scalded face in his neck.

"I remember how it feels to grow up," Miss Burke said quietly. "You think everybody is watching you, and laughing at all your mistakes, and sometimes, you don't like yourself very much." Her hand found mine in the darkness. "Be patient. One day you'll see that you're not nearly as bad as you thought."

"Grace?"

It was Pa.

"Over here, William," Miss Burke said. "We couldn't sleep."

Pa sat down beside us, his bare feet white as bones in the dark. "I thought I heard thunder."

"Will it rain tonight?" Miss Burke asked.

"I don't think so," he said, turning his face to the sky. "That lightning is a long way off. It sounds like the storm's going south of us."

I sniffed and wiped my eyes. Pa said, "Rachel? Are you all right?"

"The events of the day just caught up with her," Miss Burke said. "She'll be fine in the morning."

"Come inside, both of you," Pa said. "Time for my girls to be in bed."

Miss Burke kissed my cheek. "Sleep well, my dear."

And I did.

12

A Wedding

The next morning, Pa took Miss Burke home. John Wesley went with them so he could help Pa haul more water for the animals. They tied Miss Burke's horse behind the wagon and started out before the sun came up.

"Good-bye, Rachel!" Miss Burke called. "I'll see you Saturday."

Saturday. That was the day she and Pa would marry. There was plenty of work to be done before then. Pa made a list.

Beat the rugs and dust the furniture. Sweep the floors and polish the pots and pans. There was so much to think about and so much to do I didn't see how I would possibly finish till at least January twenty-seventh.

I rolled up the rugs and dragged them out to the clothesline and pounded them till the dirt swirled up like fog. Then I swept the floors, even the corners, and put the rugs down again. I dusted the settee, trimmed the wicks in all the lamps, and polished Mama's silver teapot.

While I worked, I tried to think of something special I could do for Pa, to show him I was sorry for all the trouble I'd caused. To show him it was all right to have a dream, even if I wasn't the center of it.

When he and John Wesley came back, I helped them roll the water barrels off the wagon. While they watered the animals, I boiled some beans, baked biscuits, and made more lemonade, not too sweet and not too sour, just the way Pa liked it.

After we ate, Pa and John Wesley made tables for the wedding feast and set them under the trees in the yard. I walked down to the blackened meadow, toward the dried-up river and the hill where a lonely wooden cross watched over my mother. Turning my face up to the sky, I closed my eyes and let all the colors come into my mind, blue and green and brown and yellow.

"Rachel?"

I nearly jumped out of my skin. "John Wesley!"

He grinned. "Whatcha doing down here?"

"Looking at a picture."

"Where?"

I pointed. "Up there. In the sky."

"You're crazy. I can't see nothing."

But I could. And it was beautiful.

When Saturday came, John Wesley got up early and came into my room carrying his new black suit and a stiff white shirt. "Do I really have to wear this?"

"I'm afraid so."

"Is Pa wearing one, too?"

"Of course, silly. He's the groom."

"How long do I hafta wear it?"

"Till Pa says you can take it off."

"How long will that be?"

"I don't know. Probably not more than a week."

The door squeaked open. "John Wesley?" Pa called out. "You up yet?"

"In here, Pa."

Pa came in and kissed my cheek. "How's my girl?"

"All right. I was thinking. After today, everything will be different. I'm scared."

He grinned. "Me, too."

"Pa, can I go feed Jake?" John Wesley bounced from one foot to the other.

"Yes, but don't be long, son. I want you dressed before the preacher gets here."

John Wesley left his new clothes on my chair and ran outside.

Pa sat on the edge of my bed and took off his spectacles. "I want to talk to you."

"What about?"

"Your mother, me, Miss Burke, everything."

"Pa, I—"

"Just a minute. I've been studying on this all week, trying to figure out the best way to say it. You'd best let me get it out now, before I get so nervous I forget every single word of it."

He raked his fingers through his hair. "First off, I know I handled this whole thing all wrong, springing Miss Burke on you like I did. I'm sorry for that. I should have prepared you and John Wesley, but I was just so happy, I thought you'd be happy, too. I didn't stop to think how it would make you feel."

Outside, John Wesley pounded along the porch, whistling for Jake.

Pa went on. "Do you remember when your mother left us? It was in April."

"I remember." Even after so many years, if I closed my eyes, I could still see the picture inside my head, of Mama's bed angled toward the meadow, her window open to the new spring unfolding on the prairie.

"She asked me to make her a promise that day, Rachel. And it nearly broke my heart to do it."

A huge knot throbbed in my throat. I couldn't bear the sorrowful look on his face. I counted the stripes on the curtain.

"She wasn't worried about dying, only about us, going through the rest of our lives alone. More than anything, she wanted you and John Wesley to have a mother to guide you."

He polished his spectacles on his sleeve and put them on again. "She made me promise to marry again someday."

I didn't know what to say.

Pa said, "I don't want you to think I'm marrying Miss Burke only on your account, though. In so many ways she reminds me of your mother. She's smart, and kind, and full of enthusiasm for life. And she loves Dakota almost as much as I do. She makes me happier than I ever thought possible. Can you understand?"

I brushed away the tears rolling down my face.

"Your mother gave me her blessing, Rachel. I wish you'd give me yours."

I couldn't stop crying. The tears poured out of me until my face felt hot and puffy and my stomach ached. Pa wrapped his arms around me and rocked me, just the way he did when I was a baby.

When I could finally talk, I told him everything. How I'd made a perfect plan to scare Miss Burke away, how the accident was all my fault, how I couldn't bear it if he loved her, and not John Wesley and me.

"You've had to grow up so fast, sometimes I forget how very young you are," Pa said. "There's a whole world of love in my heart for you and John Wesley. And for your mother, too. I won't ever forget her. Every time I see your face, or hear John Wesley's laugh, I think of her. But now I need someone to love here on earth. Maybe you can't understand it yet, but someday you will."

He stood up. "Wash your face now. I'm making pancakes."

"Are you angry with me, Pa, for causing Miss Burke's accident?"

"I had it all figured out, right from the get-go. You and Grace Burke are the two worst liars in the world," he said, smiling down at me. "Hurry now. Your pa's getting married today."

As I dressed, I could hear John Wesley outside, playing with Jake. The sun was shining, and the blue cloths Pa had spread on the wooden tables flapped in the hot wind.

"Pa, the preacher's comin'," John Wesley yelled. "And the Millers, too!" He jumped onto the porch and stuck his head through the open window. "And we haven't even had our breakfast yet."

Pa gave us our pancakes and went out to meet the preacher and Mr. and Mrs. Miller. "Come on in! We're behind schedule already. Too much excitement, I expect."

"Sounds like cold feet to me!" Mr. Miller set the brake on the wagon and jumped down. He lifted Mrs. Miller off her seat, nearly knocking off her feathered hat.

"Careful, Jacob!" she scolded. "This is my best hat."

They came inside carrying two pies and a ham. Mrs. Miller set them on the table. "You children go right on with your breakfast. I'll just sit and rest awhile."

Pa gave them some coffee and went to put on his wedding clothes. Then, while I washed our plates and tidied the kitchen, he helped John Wesley get dressed.

"Ow!" John Wesley howled. "Take it easy, Pa. You're choking me!"

"Hold still, son," Pa said. "The more you struggle, the worse it feels."

"How come Rachel doesn't have to dress up? It isn't fair."

"She's dressing up."

I wore my church dress, a yellow one with pink flowers on the skirt and a sash that tied in the back. I shined my shoes, brushed my hair and tied it back with a pink ribbon that once belonged to Mama.

Soon, two more wagons rattled up the road bringing the Olsons and the Ludke brothers with their wives and children, thirteen people laughing and singing loud enough to wake the dead. Behind them came a black buggy with a man and woman inside.

"Hey, Rachel!" John Wesley yelled. "Miss Burke's coming."

I went out to the porch with Pa, the Millers, and the preacher. The wagons creaked into the yard, scattering the chickens, and people spilled off them like ants from an anthill. While the men tended to their horses, the women came in with their applesauce cakes and roasted meats and loaves of bread still warm from their ovens.

Miss Burke's buggy drew up in the yard and the man inside helped her out. She wore a dress as blue as the Dakota sky, and a straw hat with matching ribbons that fluttered in the wind. "Everybody, this is my brother, Isaac," she said. "He's come all the way from Boston."

Isaac looked a lot like Miss Burke. He had gold hair, and eyes that were mostly gray, and a dimple in his cheek when he smiled. He shook hands with Pa and John Wesley and bowed to me like a prince at a ball.

When Miss Burke bent to kiss me, I saw the thick bandage bulging beneath the tight sleeve of her dress, and guilt settled over me like a heavy blanket. "It hardly hurts at all," she murmured. "Don't think about it anymore."

Then it was time for the wedding. We formed a circle beneath the trees and the preacher read some verses from the Bible. "Love bears all things, believes all things, hopes all things, and endures all things," he intoned. "For now we see through a glass darkly, but then, face to face."

Through a glass darkly. I remembered Mama's painting of the old gate and the misty forest on the wall at Aunt Aggie's, and how Bridey had said it was up to me to figure out what it meant. I couldn't be one hundred percent certain, but what I thought it meant was this: No matter how much you wanted to, you couldn't change what had already happened in life, and you couldn't know what would happen next. But the gate was open, and you had to walk through, and you had to trust that whatever lay beyond would be all right.

"And now abideth faith, hope, and love, these three," the preacher continued. "But the greatest of these is love."

Pa and Miss Burke stood there in the hot wind, smiling into each other's eyes. The men mopped their sweat-beaded foreheads. The ladies wept into their handkerchiefs. Miss Burke's brother swallowed hard. John Wesley tugged at his collar and stuck out his tongue, to show me he was suffocating.

Then Pa gave Miss Burke a gold ring and it was over.

Everybody cheered. The men slapped Pa on the back. The women kissed Miss Burke, then hurried to set out the food on the long tables. After we ate, the Ludkes brought out their accordions, the Olsons played their fiddles, and everyone danced till long shadows lay across the hills.

At last the preacher said, "Time to go."

He kissed Miss Burke's cheek and shook hands with Pa. "Congratulations, William. Be happy."

"Thanks. I am." Pa's arm was around her waist and she smiled up at him.

One by one, the Ludkes, the Olsons, and the Millers climbed onto their wagons and called out their good-byes. We waved till they were gone. Then came the moment I'd been waiting for. I said to Pa, "I have a present for you."

"What is it?" he asked, his eyes twinkling. "A bag of switches? A shoe full of rice?"

I brought out the picture I'd painted. Pa and Grace unwrapped it.

"Oh!" Grace said. In the last gold rays of sunlight, her gray eyes glittered.

"Well, I'll be," Pa said. "It's beautiful, honey."

"What is it?" John Wesley had already taken off his shoes and tie. "Let me see."

In the picture was our house, the red barn and the windmill, and Jake, John Wesley, and me. In the background was Mama's grave , a green rectangle beneath the shady poplar trees. I'd painted the river and the sheep grazing in a spring meadow, and the brown ribbon of road unspooling toward the horizon. In the middle of the picture I'd painted Pa. And Grace.

Grace said, "I'll ask Isaac to take it to Boston to be framed. We'll hang it above the mantel, next to your mother's portrait."

Pa kissed my cheek, and my heart brimmed, too full for words. I could feel his love spreading out like ripples on a still pond, and there was enough for all of us.

That night, the rain came. I woke to the white-hot flash of lightning, and the rumble of thunder across our parched fields. Then the first raindrops plopped onto the earth, making little craters in the dust. Faster and faster they fell, a shining silver curtain in the dark. I ran to my window to watch, and it was beautiful.

John Wesley pushed open my door and came in with his lamp.

"What are you doing out of bed?" I whispered. "You'll wake Pa and Grace."

"They're already awake," he whispered back. "Listen."

We heard laughter then, and we ran to the front window and looked out.

In the yard, Pa and Grace were barefoot in the pouring rain, turning and turning in the flickering lantern light, dancing to music only they could hear.

F
LOV

Love, D. Anne.

A year without rain

$15.15

F
LOV

Love, D. Anne.

A year without rain